D0966484

the Hike to Home

Jess Rinker

the Hike to Home

Farrar, Straus and Giroux
New York

Farrar Straus Giroux Books for Young Readers
An imprint of Macmillan Children's Publishing Group, LLC
120 Broadway, New York, NY 10271 • mackids.com

Library of Congress Cataloging-in-Publication Data
Names: Rinker, Jessica M., author.
Title: The hike to home / Jess Rinker.
Description: First edition. | New York : FSG Books for Young Readers, 2022. | Audience: Ages 10–12. | Audience: Grades 4–6. | Summary: Twelve-year-old Lin and her two new friends brave the wilderness to find a castle, prove a local legend, and discover the true meaning of home.
Identifiers: LCCN 2021045999 | ISBN 9781250812742 (hardcover)
Subjects: CYAC: Adventure and adventurers—Fiction. | Friendship—Fiction. | Freemasons—Fiction. | Bullies—Fiction. | New Jersey—Fiction. | LCGFT: Novels.
Classification: LCC PZ7.1.R57514 Hi 2022 | DDC [FIc]—dc23
LC record available at https://lccn.loc.gov/2021045999

First edition, 2022
Book design by Trisha Previte
Interior art © by Ricardo Bessa
Camera illustration by Trisha Previte
Printed in the United States of America

10 9 8 7 6 5 4 3 2 1

For Mom,
who fed me Audubon for breakfast,
maybe never realizing how it
would save my life

the Hike to Home

To awaken quite alone in a strange town is one
of the pleasantest sensations in the world.
You are surrounded by adventure.

—Freya Stark, explorer

PART ONE

1

Being thrown into public school after twelve years of basically never being around other kids is like throwing a fish in a tree to see if it will fly.

Spoiler alert: It won't.

It will hide out in the girls' bathroom taking pictures of the scribbled walls instead.

"Summer recreation camp at the middle school will be the best way for you to make friends, Lin," Dad said when we first landed here in New Jersey. "Then you'll have playmates all summer and be ready for seventh grade in the fall. How great will that be!"

Easy for him to say—the man could make friends with a porcupine. He already knows half the families on our street, and we've only been here for a month. In fact, Dad, who has a habit of going above and beyond, already offered to watch the neighbor's son every evening, a boy my age named Leo who goes to chess camp and would rather hang out with his dogs than me. I mean, I can't blame him, his dogs are *super* adorable. But Dad's attempts to help me find friends have been suffocating. Besides, I had a friend; I had Mom.

Until she decided to leave on her *own* adventure.

Now I'm two weeks in to "rec camp," which basically means playing kickball. All. Day. Long. And every day faced with the fact that I've made exactly zero "playmates." Unless you consider the wolf spider that's spinning a web in the corner of this bathroom stall a playmate.

Mom always says when you want something, you have to go for it, no matter how impossible it seems, which is why she *went for it* with this artist-residency thing she won. I tried to approach camp that way too. At first, I was interesting: the semi-famous kid from the YouTube channel *Moseying with the Mosers*. The new girl in overalls with her mom's vintage video camera.

But as soon as I opened my mouth that all changed.

I've never had a hard time talking to my parents or other adults. I've spent my whole life mostly around other grown-ups. We've always traveled too much for me to go to regular school, and I've never minded; Mom and Dad have always been the most interesting people I could have imagined. I call us the Three Musketeers. Kip, Paige, and Lin Moser: Dad is a famous home renovator, Mom a rising filmmaker star, and me, who gets to be part of everything they do.

Normally, when Dad is working on a house, and Mom isn't filming him, she and I explore new parks, hiking and learning about the local wildlife, which is my most favorite part about our adventures together. Recently she even let me start assisting her with some of her film projects. We've always been a trio. All for one, one for all. Until this summer when Mom decided to go solo. I guess, like me, she didn't see any excitement or adventure waiting for her in Newbridge, New Jersey.

Or maybe she didn't see any in me.

At least the big stall in the bathroom has a giant, cloudy-glassed window that has a ledge wide enough to sit on. I pull my knees up to my chest to try to fit perfectly in the box, but I don't quite fit. It smells a little bit like hand sanitizer and pee, but at least the windowsill is clean. There are footsteps in the hall, squeaky sneakers and shouting boys probably heading out to the field, and I sit very still until the noise passes.

I just want to get through this day and get home.

I flip through some of the photos I've taken over the past couple of weeks. I've gotten very good at sneaking pictures. I thought if I could study what other kids do in their natural habitat, maybe they would make more sense to me, but I still haven't figured out how to talk to them about normal things. I try, but every time, I get some weird looks and end up like an ostrich—head in the sand. For the record, ostriches don't actually stick their heads in sand, but it *is* what I feel like doing.

Turns out kids here don't care all that much about hiking the trails at national parks, or which wildflowers you can eat, or about what species of moth landed on them, as long as it gets *off*. They don't know about how much planning and working together as a family goes into living on the road like we do, or filming your own show, and they definitely don't know what it's like to have famous parents. And since I don't know anything about living in a small town or playing kick-ball, it's not been an easy two weeks.

And if I'm being completely honest, I haven't been trying as hard as I could to make friends, because this summer the thing I thought would never happen happened: The Three Musketeers broke up. I've spent most of the past two weeks sad about being left behind to figure this all out by myself when we were supposed to be having an adventure with Mom like we do every summer.

Why should I give her the satisfaction of making friends? Instead, I'm going to make a movie all by myself. I've learned enough from her at this point to be able to plan my own trip and film it. Even if it's just in this boring town and not the Dry Tortugas where she is. I can do my own thing too. I can *go for it* too. If she can have her own adventures, why can't I?

Looking around the confined walls of the dingy bathroom stall, which is what I imagine solitary confinement feels like, I sigh and drop my forehead to my knees. I can't even convince myself that it's possible right now.

But I'm going to try.

I aim my camera at the stall door where someone wrote in purple Sharpie and start recording:

LOVE YOURSELF, YOU'RE STUCK WITH HER TILL THE END.

Just as I'm thinking of how to use the graffiti as a clever monologue to open my movie with, the main bathroom door swings open. Voices and laughter pour into the echoey chamber. Several girls giggle about things that happened when school was still in session. What someone named Kayla did during gym class, what Jill did at lunch, what Lexi did on the bus. All they talk about is other girls. I wouldn't even know how to be part of their conversation, because I still don't really know who anybody is. Besides, it's not the kind of conversation I'm used to, or care about. If anyone wants to chat about how the most recent wildfires are endangering California's animals or who was the first woman to climb Denali, the highest mountain in the United States, I'm your girl. But I already know these girls do not want to talk to me about any of that.

I stretch a leg out, press my shoe against the stall door, and sit as still as possible. I aim my camera at my white Converse sneaker, which has the names of every place I've ever been written on it, and hold my breath, praying no one tries to open the door. Water runs as they continue to talk, and it makes a kind of cool background noise for filming dirty sneakers and the scrawl on the walls. Random words and phrases people have written all over the cinder blocks keep my camera focused.

I HATE BOYS!!!

THEY HATE YOU TOO.

GO AHEAD AND ERASE ME. I'LL BE BACK.

SIGNED, SHARPIE

The paper towel dispenser slams as someone smacks it. Purses zip open, book bags drop, and the chatter continues. There must be an army of girls out there. Through the crack in the door I see several heads of perfectly styled hair looking into the mirror. I have no idea how to blow-dry, curl, or otherwise style hair, or put on makeup. There was never any reason to, I guess, but it seems these are some things Mom and I could have learned together before sending me off into the wild completely alone.

I'm only half paying attention to their conversations until I hear:

"So what do you think about that famous YouTube girl suddenly showing up?"

"She's not famous, her parents are. She's just riding on it, thinking she's better than everyone else. She's a total snob. She won't even talk to anyone."

"Do you think she'll be in school in September?"

"Who cares."

I turn the camera off. There's a stinging sensation in my eyes and the back of my throat, but there's no way I'm going to start crying here. I swallow it back and keep one eye lined up with the crack in the door to watch them as they laugh and apply more lip gloss. I'm not a snob, really. If I were braver, I'd burst out of the stall right now and say the coolest thing that would blow their minds. But I have no idea what that is. So I stay put.

"I heard her bragging to one of the camp counselors the other day about how many viewers they have on that dumb show. What's it called? *Moseying with the Mosers*? So cringe."

I wasn't bragging, I want to scream at them. The counselor *asked* me about it.

"If she were smart she'd keep her mouth shut. No one wants to hear about all the places she's been in that dumb converted bus."

I clench my jaw so tightly it hurts. Through the crack in the door I see one girl apply mascara. Another rolls her eyes.

"Total show-off."

Someone else chimes in and finally takes the subject off me. I can breathe a little better.

"Oh my god, you guys! Are you allowed to go to Michael Sanders's Fourth of July party?"

The voices continue on about how cute Michael is, whoever he is, and then fade as they all pick up their bags and shuffle back out. Lunch is over, and it's time for the afternoon game of, you guessed it, kickball. Never in a million years would I think I'd want to stay indoors, but kickball and soccer and whatever other game they make us play have proved reason enough. I'd rather stick my head in this toilet and flush. Twice. I rest my head against the wall and loudly sigh. *Thank god that's over.*

Fish, meet birds.

They all take off without you.

Next to me, a stall door creaks opens. "They're all gone! You can come out now," a sweet-sounding voice tells me. At first, I don't move. I don't know if I can take any more. How are you supposed to know who to trust around here?

"It's okay," the voice says. I can hear a light tapping on my stall door. "Don't listen to anything they say. The only excitement they can muster in their boring lives is to make fun of other girls, but we're not all like that. My name's Tinsley Cooper. You're Lin, right?"

I hop off the windowsill, open my door, and come face-to-face with a girl with bright pink curly hair, wearing a black-and-red lace dress and black boots. I can't help but smile and take in her whole ensemble.

"*Cabaret*," she says, pulling at the ruffles on her dress. "It's a musical. Anyway, hi!"

"I didn't know anyone else was in here," I say. I've definitely noticed her over the past several days. Her outfits are pretty spectacular, and I've seen her in the athletic fields, often singing as she plays whatever game we're mandated to play each day like her life is a musical. One morning she came to camp wearing a boy's wig and a Carhartt coverall, and everyone called her the janitor, but she kept on singing something about seizing the day. Clearly she's way braver than I am, which makes me wonder how she got that way. How does she not let the other kids' words bother her?

"How'd you know it was me?" I ask.

She nods. "Recognized your scribbled Converse before you jumped up. I came in to pee right in front of that gang of perfume and hair." She touches her own curly head. "I should talk. But then I didn't want to make any noise, and now I don't have to go anymore." She shrugs and walks over to the sink to wash her hands. "Don't worry about any of them. They talk a lot, but they're harmless. They're just jealous."

I start packing up my stuff, throw away my paper lunch bag. "Yeah, I guess so."

"*Moseying with the Mosers* is so fun," Tinsley says. "My family and I watch it all the time. My dad also works on houses." She looks in the mirror and adjusts a few curls, but they simply spring back into place. "Or did, anyway."

"Thanks," I say. I don't really want to talk about it, though. I'm *not* a show-off like those girls said, and it just makes me think of Mom and what my life is supposed to look like right now.

"What's the video camera for?" she asks.

I throw my backpack up on my shoulders and hold on to the camera strap. "It's my mom's. But I've been using it to . . ." I pause, a little afraid to tell the truth, but then think Tinsley is probably the kind of person who would like this. "Make a movie about my summer," I say.

"That's so cool!" Tinsley says, tossing her crumpled paper towel in the trash. "Can I be in it?" We push out of the bathroom together and walk toward the big double doors at the end of the hall.

"Sure," I say. "Once I figure out what it's actually about." Through the windows we can see other kids gathering in the field.

"I *despise* kickball," Tinsley says, reading my mind. "If we ask the counselor to walk around the track instead, they'll let us and we can just talk."

"Really? You want to keep talking with me?"

Tinsley has a funny surprised look on her face, but then she grins. "Yeah, why wouldn't I?"

And that was the first time Tinsley Cooper saved my life.

I was raised on national and state parks like most kids are raised on Dr. Seuss. So far, my favorite park is in Arizona, a place called the Wave that you can only get to by permit and looks like you're walking on another planet. Red waves of sandstone surround you like a fiery dream. It was one of my mom's and my first smaller trips together, where we collaborated like real cofilmmakers. After that she let me be part of all her projects. Yellowstone, the Rocky Mountains, the Grand Tetons, everywhere she went, I got to help. I thought it would be the same for every expedition she went on, until she left me behind with Dad. For turtles.

Don't get me wrong, Dad is great. We get along fine and all. He's just not Mom. He can't go on adventures, because his job has such long days. He's the builder, the planner, the scheduler. He's amazing at what he does, but he has to stay on-site to work his magic.

Mom would say things like, "Hey, Lin, let's skip this afternoon's math textbook lesson and head over to the wildflower meadow instead." And then we'd get there and she'd end up teaching me something like the golden ratio, how mathematical patterns show up in nature, and I'd end up learning without even realizing it. I thought we were best friends, but best friends don't ditch each other.

This summer Dad could have taken a job in any adventurous-sounding state—*The Mountain State* of West Virginia, or Alaska: *The Last Frontier*. Or New Mexico: *The Land of Enchantment*, which is the coolest name for a state that could ever exist. Towns *apply* to have Dad come and restore an old home; he gets to choose the state we visit. Originally we were supposed to end up in Oregon. Its motto is "She flies with her own wings." How freaking cool is that? Dad got a job in Portland, and Mom and I were going to check out Crater Lake National Park and film the collapsed volcano for her next project. But instead my life collapsed: Dad's job fell through, and Mom won the artist residency and left me behind.

This time, no adventurous state for us. Dad ended up choosing a new job to flip an ancient purple Victorian home in New Jersey of all stupid places. *The Garden State*. What kind of adventure is in a garden? I guess he figured it was better to have a lot of other people around to help him out with me this summer. Little does he know I do not want help. I only wanted Mom.

On the way home from camp, I film the uneven sidewalks and mature maple trees that line the streets. In my mind, I practice what I'm going to say to Dad about quitting summer camp, because despite the great afternoon with Tinsley, I really don't want to go back. That place is just not me; it's none of the things I enjoy doing, and Tinsley and I can't walk the track all day, every day.

He's going to ask, "What will you do all summer?" But I have a plan, a list of things that I'll enjoy and he'll support. I'll go to the library and sign up for summer reading, and maybe I could start a job as a dog walker. If Leo would talk to me, I could practice with his dogs. Though, after today in the bathroom, I wonder if my time would be better spent watching a lot of YouTube to catch up on hair and makeup tips to learn how to be a proper thirteen-year-old before my birthday in the fall. Just thinking about those girls makes it hard to breathe. How will I ever be ready for real school if I can't even handle a few weeks of camp?

I hear someone humming, turn off the camera, and see Tinsley Cooper jogging to catch up to me. "Hey!" she says. "Can I walk with you?"

"Yeah," I say. "Of course."

"Cool. I wanted to ask you before, but I wasn't sure if you wanted company."

"Oh? Why'd you think that?"

"You usually leave the school really fast." As Tinsley walks, the ruffles on the hem of her dress bounce. "And you seem kind of serious, like you're walking death row."

I snort-laugh. "Sorry." I'm sure I do look pretty serious,

considering every day I've been plotting an escape from camp, or more accurately an escape from my entire life situation right now.

"And, honestly," she says, "I was kind of afraid since you're so famous, you wouldn't be interested in talking to me."

Funny that I was thinking it was the other way around. I kick a stone and send it flying down the sidewalk. "That's definitely not true. And I'm not really that famous; my dad is the real star."

Her face seems to light up. "Do you think I could meet him?"

"My dad?"

She nods. My heart sinks a little bit. If she only wants to be friends because of my dad, that would suck. "Sure," I say. "Come on over."

At least Dad would be happy I finally *had* a friend. And maybe he'd stop pushing Leo on me. Because I've tried. And Leo Martin is a whole other story.

Leo is the shiest person I've ever known in my life. His mom is like the most extreme opposite of my mom, but apparently they knew each other in high school so of course my parents were totally on board to help her out. Ms. Martin never lets Leo stay home alone, texts him constantly to make sure he's okay, and basically treats him like he's five. But she's also very nice, and when we first moved here, she brought us a homemade meat-sauce lasagna to welcome us to the neighborhood. Mom didn't have the heart to tell her we're vegetarians. So we scraped the hamburger out of it and just ate the pasta.

But ever since then, Leo has stayed at our house each day after his chess camp at the local college, which is across town. He goes by bus, and apparently the entire day is spent inside playing board games and chess. Don't get me wrong, I love games, but for, like, rainy days and stuff. Who wants to spend their entire summer inside?

Tinsley and I reach the Victorian where our big converted bus is parked on the side yard. Leo is already there, lying on the bench holding a book up in the air to block the sun as he reads. His usual position, his usual book—*The Sword in the Stone*. His fluffy dogs, Merlin and Little John, run over to us, tails wagging. Unlike Leo, they are very social.

"Aww," Tinsley croons. "You guys are so cute!"

The dogs wiggle and weave around our legs for a minute while we give them scratches, and then trot back over to Leo.

Tinsley waves. "Hi, Leo!"

He sort of nods and goes back to reading.

"Good luck there," I say under my breath, so Leo can't hear. "I keep trying to start conversations with him, but they don't get very far."

"Yeah, sounds like Leo," Tinsley says. "Don't worry, it's not you. So your dad's in there?" She points to the purple house, and I lead her over to meet the star. Dad is inside hacking away at something; I can hear the scream of the saw before we reach the door. I peek my head in and wave so he knows I'm home. He and two other guys are working on the fancy trim around the windows. They both give me a little wave.

"Hey, hon!" Dad shouts over the blasting saw. Sawdust sprinkles over his dark curly hair like giant pieces of dandruff, but he still looks handsome. He always does. Mom says it's the main reason their YouTube channel took off. I told her to please not talk about Dad like that around me, it's gross. But it is the truth. He turns heads when he walks down the street. It's totally disgusting.

"Hi, Dad. This is Tinsley Cooper," I shout. "She goes to the camp I used to go to but quit today."

Dad cuts the saw and tilts his head at me. "Oh really?" he says. "We'll talk about that later." He pushes his googles up on his head. Sawdust goes everywhere, and Tinsley giggles. He comes over and shakes her hand. "Nice to meet you, Tinsley. That's an unusual name. Like tinsel on a Christmas tree. What does it mean?"

"Dad," I warn. He's always saying embarrassing things. But Tinsley doesn't seem to mind. She bounces a little bit on her toes.

"I don't even know," she says. "I think my parents just liked the way it sounded."

"All right, well, very nice to meet you. I'll be out in a few!" He waves and gets back to pushing the screeching saw across the table.

We head back to our bus, our home on wheels and the coziest place in the world. I give Tinsley the grand tour, which is actually quite short. My parents designed and built the entire thing so that everything folds into corners and can be used for multiple purposes, so my bed is a loft on one side, and underneath is a desk that can be folded up for more space. The way back of the bus is a private room for my parents, and the kitchen table turns into a guest bed. People don't realize how much space we actually have. The white wood-paneled walls make it bright and happy. We even have houseplants.

"This is about the coolest thing I've ever seen," Tinsley says. "You are so lucky."

"Thanks. I love it," I say, which is usually true. It never feels crowded, and we have everything we need. The best is when there's a hard rain beating on the metal roof. No matter where we go I've always felt at home, but now without Mom it feels cavernous and too quiet. "It seems small, but it's actually way bigger than our old RV."

"I think it seems awesome." Tinsley peers at a family photo on the fridge. "You look just like your mom. She's so pretty."

No one has ever called me pretty, except Mom and Dad, who have to say that. "Thanks. I have Dad's hair, though." I pull out a glass container from the shelf over the stove. "Do you like fried plantains?"

"I've never had them," she says, and sits at the table. There's a package on it, and she spins it around toward me. "This is for you."

"Oh, cool." It's sent from Amazon. I rip it open, and there's a book and a little gift note: *Lin, you'll love this story. She reminds me of you, my future mountaineer. Miss you! Mom*

The book is a biography about a woman named Annie Smith Peck, a mountain climber from the nineteenth century, a time when women did not climb mountains. On a normal afternoon, I'd sit out in the hammock on the edge of the yard and gobble this up. But with a guest here, that would probably be rude. I hand it to Tinsley so she can see it. "My mom and I do a lot of hiking."

Tinsley takes the book and glances at the back cover. "This lady did way more than hiking. We're talking massive mountains. She was a suffragist too."

I dig through the cabinets for the peanut butter while Tinsley flips through the pages and reads random facts about Annie out loud. "Says she was born in 1850, and broke all kinds of climbing records."

As Tinsley reads more about the woman's life, Annie Smith Peck actually reminds me a lot of *Mom*, even more than me. I feel like I'm mostly along for the ride; Mom plans all the adventures. And Annie planned *epic* adventures. She set out on her own climbing expeditions constantly and became famous in her time. Only she never married, and never had kids.

I set the peanut butter jar on the table and show Tinsley how I dip a fried plantain. "Best combo ever," I say. As we snack, Tinsley reads more facts about how Annie constantly set out on expeditions alone, which for a woman is unusual even today, but especially that long ago. I wonder what gave Annie the courage to do it. Whatever it was, Mom clearly has it too. The bigger question is, do I? Could I set out on an adventure all by myself?

"Don't you think so?"

I suddenly hear Tinsley over my self-pity daydream. "Oh, sorry, don't I think what?"

"That this Annie lady is badass?"

"Totally." I realize we haven't offered anything to Leo, so I get up and slide the window over the sink open. "Do you want anything to eat?" I shout down to him. "I have some leftover fried plantains and peanut butter."

Leo shakes his head but doesn't look up. "I'm allergic to peanut butter."

I knew that. "Right. Just plantains, then?"

"No thanks," he says but doesn't take his eyes off the book. He pushes up his glasses and acts like I'm not staring at him through the screen. I slam the window shut. It's louder than I meant it to be, but oh well. I also regret shutting it because the bus gets stuffy very quickly.

"Don't take it personally," Tinsley says. "He doesn't talk much to anyone. I've known Leo since kindergarten, and all he's ever done is *read*." She rolls her eyes way up to the ceiling.

I pick up my mom's camera and click through some of the footage I got earlier. "I noticed. I thought maybe it was me." If the girls in the bathroom thought it, why not Leo too?

Tinsley shakes her head. "Nah. He's just quiet. So what's your movie going to be about?"

I aim the camera at her, and she tilts her head, fans her fingers around her face, and grins for me. "I haven't been able to figure out what yet. Normally when my mom isn't filming my dad, she and I find a cool park to explore. She's really good at finding places. But there's not much around here to do," I say.

"You can say that again." Tinsley closes Annie's book and sighs. "Compared to what you and your family usually do, Newbridge must seem like a joke. So who's filming the show now?"

"No one. It's sort of on a break because my mom's away." Looking out the window, I see Dad come out of the house and shake his hair. Dust flies everywhere as he crosses the yard and stops at the table to say hi to Leo. Leo smiles a lot when Dad talks to him. He even sits up and looks at him directly. Dad always seems to have that effect on people. Charming, Mom would say. I can't hear what they're saying, though, so I slide the window open again.

"Supposed to be a supermoon this weekend!"

"What's a supermoon?" Leo asks.

"It's when the moon is closest to the earth, so it looks way bigger than normal. Happens a few times a year. I was thinking about taking Lin on a moonlit hike on Saturday. Would you be interested in joining us?"

Leo shifts on the bench. "Maybe. I'll have to ask my mom."

"Of course," Dad says. "We'd love to have you." He shakes

his hair out one more time and steps up into the bus. "Hey, Lindy-Lin. Tinsel-toes."

Tinsley laughs like it's the best joke she's ever heard.

"Hey, Dad," I say abruptly. "So, we're going hiking this weekend?" Dad is normally too busy to take days off for stuff like that.

"I was thinking it might be fun. If you want to? The park map is in the drawer by the toaster if you want to take a look. You too, Tinsel-toes," he says. "I mean, I know I'm not Mom—"

"No, I mean yes! Definitely! Let's do it. But good luck getting—" I gesture my thumb toward the window and then pull out the map.

"Gotta give everyone a chance," Dad whispers. "Besides, you two will never become friends if you keep hiding out in here and he keeps hiding out in that book."

There he goes again. "I know, you've mentioned that," I say while staring at the map, which is pretty basic compared to some trails I've been on. Waterfalls, overlooks, campground, service roads. All your typical stuff. But still it looks cool, and it would be fun to do something with Dad.

I toss the map back in the drawer. "Are you done for the day?"

"No, I had to come grab a manual for the saw. Got it jammed. Couple more hours and then I'll get the grill lit, okay? We're going to do those stuffed peppers tonight. I'll prep them now, and then you'll have to entertain yourself just a little while longer." He disappears into the back of the bus and then emerges with a pamphlet, sets it on the table, and washes his hands. "I know—you two could take some cash and see if Leo wants to go get ice cream or something."

Tinsley stands up. "I'd love to go get ice cream, but I actually have to get home. I relieve my mom from Dad duty so she can get a break."

"Dad duty?" I ask her.

She shakes her head, as if remembering something. "I forgot, you're new here. He works for Sanders Construction, and he fell off a ladder months ago. Messed up his back really bad. Basically, he has to have someone around every day, and right now that someone is my mom." Tinsley looks at my dad. "He, um, he actually wanted to apply to be on your crew, Mr. Moser, when we all first found out you were coming here."

"Tinsley," Dad says, "that's awful. I'm so sorry to hear this. I'm sure I'd have hired him in a heartbeat. You let us know if there's ever anything we can do to help your family out."

She smiles. "Sure. I'll see you tomorrow, maybe?" she asks.

"Yeah. Definitely," I say. "I'm really sorry about your dad. I hope he's better soon." I can't imagine if something like that happened to my dad—renovation is his whole life. I imagine it's the same for Tinsley's dad.

"Thanks. He should be. It's just a long recovery. See ya!" She leaves and waves goodbye to Leo, who, once again, simply nods.

After she leaves, I turn to Dad. "Please don't make me go back to camp."

"Explain," Dad says as he pulls two green peppers out of the fridge and hands them to me for washing. "You just made a nice friend, and now you don't want to go back?"

I tell him as much as possible without getting into the dirty details of the bathroom, and he seems to get it.

"I was really hoping it would be a good thing for you, Lin, but I'm not going to force you. Hopefully we'll get a refund. But you will have a lot of days to occupy yourself."

I rinse the peppers in the cool water and toss them back so he can cut out the centers. "I know. I can. Camp was just awful. Maybe instead, I could film your work, for the YouTube channel? I mean, *someone* should, since Mom just quit."

Dad looks at me seriously. "Lin. Your mother did not quit." He gets a bigger knife out and starts chopping an onion. "She got the opportunity of a lifetime to do this film residency; she couldn't turn it down."

I pull a can of black beans out of the cabinet and set it down on the table a little too hard. "Her life is here, with us."

Dad puts the knife down. "Her life is a lot of things, just like mine is, just like yours will be. Besides, I have no problem breaking from the show this year. Sometimes all that fanfare takes my focus off the project. It's nice to work without the pressure."

He assembles the stuffed peppers while I sit at the table drumming my fingers. When he's done, he wraps them in foil and sticks them in the fridge for later. Then he picks the saw manual back up and taps me on the head with it. "It's summer. Go be a kid. Go explore."

"There's nothing in Newbridge, New Jersey, to explore, Dad."

"Have you even tried yet?"

"No. It's boring."

"No Moser child could ever be bored."

"Considering I'm the only Moser child and I'm bored here, that proves you wrong."

Dad gives me a look.

I know when I'm coming close to a line with my parents, and this is it. I'm not risking him sending me back to camp. "Fine. I'll go explore this dinky town. I'm sure I could find more footage for my documentary, *One Terrible Summer*."

I'm proud of myself for coming up with such a perfect title, but Dad doesn't take the bait. He sighs and says, "Wear the strap and just be careful with that camera."

"I always am."

"I know you're responsible. I just have to say that. It's part of parental law and order." He winks at me. "Go find some adventure! Start with ice cream! And lose that negative tone."

He ducks out of the bus, messes Leo's hair as he walks by, and heads back into the Victorian.

The mason jar under the sink has about thirty dollars of what we call "fun money." I take ten and step out of the bus into the hot, late-day sun. It really is a perfect afternoon to go get ice cream. But I'm not telling Dad he had a good idea. Besides, I don't even know if it's going to work yet. Leo is a hard case to crack.

But Annie Smith Peck never saw a mountain she couldn't climb.

So, here goes nothing.

3

Leo's book blocks his face when I come out of the bus. I kneel down and pet his dogs. Merlin is brown and white and always alert and serious, and Little John, who's anything but little, is almost all black, and more likely to be lying on his back for a belly rub. But they are super sweet and soft and follow Leo around everywhere without a leash. "They're such good boys," I say, trying to sound as confident as my dad, like I start conversations every day. "How long have you had them?"

Slowly he lowers the book so I can only see his dark brown eyes through his glasses. He seems surprised and doesn't respond at first. I raise my eyebrows, and he sets the book down and says, "They . . . they're Australian shepherds and very smart. My mom rescued them a couple years ago and trained them both from puppies."

"I bet you named them, right? From the King Arthur stories?"

His face brightens. But "Yeah" is all he says.

I sit on the bench across from him and pick up his book,

which is worn and bendy. "I've read this one too. Looks like you've read it a lot."

He nods and says, "I reread it every summer."

"Wow. That's a commitment," I say, and then hold up the ten and ask, "So, my dad gave me some money. Want to go get ice cream with me?"

He says nothing. *Who says nothing to ice cream?*

"I mean, you're not allergic to it, are you?"

"No," he says. "Only to bees and peanuts. And shrimp. And some antibio . . ." He trails off, maybe realizing he's spoken too many words out loud, and his freckled cheeks turn pink. I've heard being shy can be like an affliction. That's got to change. If we're going to be spending the whole long, terrible summer together, then we're going to spend it my way. Even if "my way" was actually my dad's idea.

"Come on," I say. "It'll be fun. I'm going to take pictures and maybe a little video for my film." I hold up the camera. "Have you always lived here?"

Leo nods, but he doesn't look at me, and bends to pet Merlin and Little John instead. A bright orange-and-black butterfly lands on the table, flaps its wings a couple of times, and then lifts up and away.

"Good," I say. "Then you can help me get to know the town better."

"What is your movie about, anyway?" he asks, still looking at the dogs.

I can't believe he's asked me a question. *Do not word-vomit all over Leo. Whatever you do, do not tell him he just missed a viceroy butterfly that everyone thinks is a monarch but is actually a look-alike. Don't scare him away like the girls at camp.*

"Well"—I clear my throat—"I wanted to do something a little more exciting, but I think it's just going to be a film about my first summer trying to be a 'normal' kid." I use my fingers as air quotes around *normal*. "I've decided to call it *One Terrible Summer*."

"Is that what you really think?" he asks, looking up at my face for the first time. "That being normal is terrible?"

He looks a little hurt, and I realize he probably thinks I think *he's* normal. "Don't worry! I don't think you're normal." *Wait, that's not right.* "I mean, you are normal, but you're a good normal, not a bad normal. I'm talking about, like, going from an exciting life traveling to a boring life in a small, uninteresting—"

Leo raises his eyebrows and blinks.

I'm an idiot. "I'll stop talking now. I'm sorry."

"It's okay. I think I get it." Leo nods toward my camera. "That thing looks really old. Can't you use your phone?"

Thankful he seems to have forgiven me for insulting his entire existence, I try to tone it down a bit and not say anything that will make him think I'm weird. "It is kind of old, but that's what makes it fun. It makes me feel like a movie director from the nineties." And of course, I say exactly the kind of cringe thing my dad would say. "It takes both photographs and videos and it's also way easier to hold. And doesn't lose a charge ridiculously fast the way a phone does."

Leo puts his book in his bag. "I like it."

Whew. "So, you'll go to town with me?"

Leo looks over to the purple house as if an excuse will walk out the front door and save him. But then he surprises me. "Yes. I just need to stop at home first and put these two and my bag in the house."

Inside I'm screaming with victory. *Am I actually making a friend and doing normal friend things all by myself?* On the outside I simply clear my throat and calmly say, "Okay."

It seems Leo runs out of words, because he doesn't say anything else on the walk to his house. I don't say anything either, because I don't want to press my luck and risk him changing his mind. He brings the dogs and his bag inside, and we continue on our silent walk toward town. We pass a Sunoco gas station, Galasso's Pizza, and a cute coffee shop called Common Grounds.

Eventually, though, I can't handle the silence anymore. "So . . . what do you think of Tinsley Cooper?"

Leo shrugs. "She's nice, but she makes me a little nervous."

I almost laugh, but I can totally see what he's saying. She's definitely a lot different from most kids with all the costumes and outfits she wears, that bright pink curly hair and those icy-blue eyes. Pretty striking actually. Maybe Leo *likes* likes her.

"I think she seems cool," I say as we continue on. "Like a bright pink butterfly."

"I've never seen a pink butterfly," he says.

"Because they don't exist," I say.

Leo gives me a really weird look. Oh no. That might have been too much. I turn on the video camera and film the houses as we walk, trying to sound casual. "Pink isn't really a color by itself, so people say it can't be found in nature. They say that it's always a combo of colors, or a trick of the eye, not its own thing."

"Right." Leo shoves his hands in his pockets.

"Anyway, it's a phrase my mom uses for something rare and beautiful—it's a 'pink butterfly.' I'm just full of random useless information," I say, trying to make a joke of it now. Adults are always impressed, but maybe other kids aren't. How am I supposed to know?

"No, it's cool, I just didn't get it."

My face feels hot as we turn the corner onto Bridge Street. I aim my camera on the bright green sign for Dilly's Ice Cream a couple of blocks up as I try to think of something not quite so nerdy to talk about, something Leo will like. But I can't come up with anything.

"You're really shy, aren't you?" I ask. And then realize I've gone and done it again! That's probably the *worst* thing to ask a shy person. "I'm sorry. I'm not used to talking to other people my own age."

"I noticed." He laughs but not in an unkind way.

"I don't mind," I say as we squeeze past a small group of older ladies carrying paper shopping bags. "That you're shy, I mean."

He looks at me, even though I have the camera facing him, and says, "Thanks. I don't know if I'm shy or if I just haven't found the right people to talk to yet."

I stop recording and let the camera hang around my neck. "I haven't even told my parents this, but you know this dumb day camp my dad signed me up for? Well, I've been eating lunch in the girls' bathroom so I wouldn't have to sit near anyone in the cafeteria." I blurt it all out thinking maybe Leo would get it.

He squints his eyes. "That's kind of gross."

Maybe I was wrong. "I didn't know where else to be alone!"

"Why, though?" Leo asks. "You don't seem shy. At all."

"I'm not, usually. But I've never really hung out with other kids. Only adults."

"Ever?" Leo asks.

"Ever. Some of the girls at camp made me feel like it's better for me not to open my mouth at all."

Leo nods. "You might be too adventurous for them."

"What do you mean?"

"This is a small town where literally nothing ever happens. If a dog poops in someone's yard, it's big news. You have a very different life."

Or *had*, I think, *until Mom decided I wasn't interesting anymore and took off on her own expedition*. Now I'm stuck in a town where poop is news.

"There has to be *something* exciting about Newbridge," I say as we step inside the cold ice cream shop. A warm, toasty-sweet smell fills my nose. Waffle cones. "Something worth taking pictures of or filming or something! An art museum, even."

"Dilly's is about it," Leo says. We both order mint chocolate chip waffle cones. I add hot fudge, and he adds whipped cream and sprinkles. And then we are back out in the heat, eating as fast as we can. "The park by the river is nice too," he says. "Have you been there yet?"

"No, I haven't," I say. Which is weird for me, but I've hardly explored anything yet. To be honest, I didn't think there'd be anything here worth exploring.

"I'll show you."

As we walk, Leo talks more about some of the things about town he really likes. He seems more relaxed with me the more we talk, like we've known each other longer than just a few weeks. It's actually not that hard to talk to Leo after all. Hopefully he feels the same about me.

When we reach the park, I'm already done with my ice cream, so I take some photos of the river and people on benches far in the distance. I record some video of people throwing a Frisbee. One couple is walking a dog. I envision it as the "before" footage, like in a zombie movie before everyone starts turning, but before what in my own movie, I have no idea. I'm about to ask Leo if he'll let me take some video of him now, but he suddenly says, "You know what, there is one kind of cool thing about Newbridge you might be interested in. Well, if you could find it."

"What?"

Leo leads us to a bench under a giant sugar maple. "Pen's Castle."

"Interesting. Tell me more."

He seems hesitant to say anything else, and I'm sure it's because he's afraid of embarrassing himself, just the way I felt sitting in that stupid toilet stall and hearing what those girls really thought about me. He takes a breath. "It's just a legend. People call it the 'Castle in the Clouds' sometimes. It's probably not even true. I shouldn't have mentioned it."

"A castle in the clouds? Like in the sky? Definitely not true."

Leo shrugs and looks at his ice cream. I think I might have offended him. "I'm sorry, I didn't mean it like that," I say.

"It's not in the sky," he says. "It's just supposed to be way up in the hills. Abandoned somewhere off the Appalachian Trail and built into the cliffside overlooking the river and all of Pennsylvania."

That sounds more likely. I turn to face him. "For real?"

He sucks melted ice cream out of the bottom of the cone. "It's more of a rumor . . . No one's ever seen it. But it's supposed to be old, like hundreds of years."

"So you don't know if it's *really* real."

"No one does, but it's Newbridge's most famous claim to . . . well, anything."

"That's weird. When I searched online before we moved here, nothing that interesting came up." In fact, the only thing I'd found about Newbridge was a basic town page and under "Things to Do" it had a couple of festivals and a walking tour of old homes. Dad's kind of thing, but not mine.

Leo sighs. "Okay, well, it's not *that* famous. You won't find much online about it. People *used* to come looking for it, but not so much anymore."

It seems to me Leo's story keeps morphing. "So a famous myth to Newbridge but not really anyone else."

"Yeah." Leo's shoulders slump a little bit. I can tell he was trying to impress me, and now I feel bad for not being impressed.

"Maybe not as cool as I thought," he says. "When I was little I was super into it because some people say it was built by a descendant of King Arthur."

Now *that's* impressive. I can't help my mouth from dropping open. "You mean like your book? Arthur and the Knights of the Round Table, the sword in the stone, and all that?" My mom first read that one to me when I was younger. She always read to me, even long after I could read for myself. It was my favorite thing to do with her around a campfire. "That's pretty wild," I say.

"It's probably not true," Leo says, "but I always thought it would be amazing to try to go find it."

There's a spark of something I recognize inside me, the first I've felt it since we moved here. *Now that's an idea*. I turn to Leo, bringing my leg up on the bench, and lean toward him, which makes him back up just a tiny bit, so I sit up straight. Mom says some people need more personal space than others, but sometimes I forget when I'm excited. "This would make the best movie ever. Can you even imagine? Forget *One Terrible Summer*. I'll call it *Climbing to the Castle in the Clouds*. I *have* to go up there."

He leans back a little bit more as though even my voice is too close to his face. "I've always wanted it to be true, but no one has ever found it." He bites the waffle cone and a bit crumbles. "It's a little sketchy."

"Can I please record you saying that?" I clasp my hands together, pleading. "It's perfect—the naysayer at the beginning of the expedition."

"I'm not going on any expedition."

"It's just for my movie, it doesn't matter." I give him my best pleading face.

"Fine," he says.

"You're the best, Leo." I turn on the camera and begin to record.

Lin: *So, tell us, Leo Martin, the castle is rumored to be over a hundred years old. Any idea why no one has found it yet?*

Leo: *No.*

Lin: *Any idea how the secret has been kept for so long?*

Leo: *No.*

Lin: *You've lived in Newbridge your whole life, and you have no theories?*

Leo: *No.*

I turn off the camera. "This isn't working. You have to sound a *little* more interested. A little more . . . alive."

He shrugs. "I don't have TV experience like you do."

"I don't have TV experience."

"Sure you do—*Moseying with the Mosers*? I've seen—"

I turn all the way to face him and try to hide my smile. "You've watched my parents' show?" For some reason it didn't occur to me that Leo would care.

He pushes up his glasses and looks away. "Not really. I mean, I just checked it out because my mom was going on and on about you guys moving here and how she knew your mom from childhood. She couldn't get enough of it."

Leo's gaze is pulled across the park toward a group of boys playing basketball. "You have a really amazing life, Lin," he says. "I don't blame you for thinking this town is boring."

"I'm reconsidering my first impression," I say. "You've really never tried to find that castle?" I ask. "Even though you love the King Arthur story so much that you read it every summer?"

"I wouldn't have a clue where to start. It's not like there's a map or anything. And I'm definitely not roaming around the woods by myself." A large drop of melted ice cream lands on his thigh. I hand him an extra napkin.

"What about your mom? Can't you go hiking together?"

He shakes his head as he tries to wipe the ice cream off his shorts. "Hiking is definitely not her thing."

I never really thought parents and kids might not always

love doing the same things like me and Mom. It's a little different with Dad, but I still always get really excited when he wants to do something outdoorsy, and he seems proud when I watch him work. I feel bad Leo doesn't have someone to do the things he likes, but that's where friends come into play, and I think we're becoming just that. *Was it really as easy as going for ice cream?* Add Tinsley to the mix and what a great team we would be when seventh grade starts—we can walk to school together and share a table at lunch. Three fish who could stick together no matter what.

"Uh-oh," Leo suddenly says, breaking me out of my daydream.

"Don't worry, it'll come out in the wash," I say. But then I realize he's not looking at the stain on his shorts anymore, he's looking across the park in the direction of three older boys. Leo tosses the last bit of his waffle cone in the trash, grabs my hand—and then quickly lets go when he realizes he's touching me—and says, "We have to go. Now."

"What's the matter?" I glance again at the boys, who seem to be heading right in our direction, and follow Leo out of the park.

Leo jogs ahead of me. "The Sanders brothers and their minion, Seth Dolan."

"Who are the Sanders brothers?"

"Aaron and Michael Sanders. The older one is Aaron." As we weave through people on the sidewalk, Leo fills me in. "Their family owns half this town. And their dad pays off anyone standing in their way. Not even kidding. They have an older brother who crashed a car once, and their dad cleaned it up before cops showed up—he'd been drinking. They literally never get in trouble for anything."

"Okay, but why are we running from them?" For being small, Leo's surprisingly fast. I hold the camera close so it doesn't bang against my chest as we jog behind Holiday Hardware and down a narrow alley. Leo ducks behind a dumpster, and I get the feeling this isn't the first time he's done so.

"Because I got them in trouble at the end of school," he whispers. "And now they want revenge." He leans around to try to get a better look in the direction we came from. I do the same and immediately feel like I have to pee. The greasy dumpster smells like sour milk and old boiled cabbage. I try not to touch it. The name *Sanders* is familiar. Didn't Tinsley just say something about her dad and Sanders?

"Bad hiding place, dingus," a deep voice says from the other side, startling us both. "Who's your girlfriend?"

I look up into the eyes of Aaron Sanders, whose hard, angry face totally ruins his good looks, and glance at Leo, who's so pale he looks green. At least now I know why Leo wasn't all that excited about coming to town. It suddenly hits me: Sanders Construction. Tinsley's dad must work for this kid's dad. Or used to.

Dad said go look for adventure. Seems like it found me first.

We're trapped between the building and the dumpster, and this is an experience I, for one, have never had. So, can't say Newbridge is totally boring anymore, because this is anything but boring. Aaron, Michael, and Seth block the only way out. And they seem pretty happy about this predicament. Leo, on the other hand, has now skipped green and gone gray. He looks like he might throw up. I wonder what these boys have done to him.

"What do you want?" I ask, trying to sound the least afraid possible. It's not easy.

"What makes you think we want anything?" the younger brother, Michael, says. He looks a lot like Aaron, both sandy-blond and strong, but with a bigger forehead. Seth is the complete opposite of the two of them—black hair and light eyes, really skinny, and nowhere near as much anger in his face. In fact, he looks a little confused as to why they're even standing here surrounding us.

"If you don't want anything, then kindly move out of the

way so my friend and I can go home." I stand and try to pull Leo up with me. He's a little shaky on his feet.

"If you don't mind, we have some business with *your friend*," says Michael. He has the meanest look on his face, but I realize he has no idea who I am. That's new.

Leo looks at me, unblinking. These are the first kids to not recognize me. I have to admit, despite the circumstances, I kind of like it. I could be anybody right now. Not the weird girl at camp, not a know-it-all, and not YouTube famous. Just a normal, small-town girl. Or, better yet, someone who knows exactly how to deal with bullies to make them go away. I could save the day with one snarky line or karate kick to the shin. If only I knew karate.

But before I can think of what to do or say, a woman comes down the alley: our chance to escape. I stand up straight and talk really loud and enthusiastic like we were all in on some kind of game together. "Okay, guys, well, that was super fun. We have to head home, but we'll see you tomorrow!"

Aaron tries to protest, but then he also sees the woman approaching and has to go along with my act. As I figured, the boys step aside, pretend nothing happened, and let us pass. We speed-walk down the alley and don't slow down until we're almost home, but I can't help but grin over our successful getaway.

Out of breath, I ask, "What in the world was that about?"

He shakes his head. "Doesn't matter."

"Is this why you don't like to go to town?"

Leo stops and throws his hands up in the air. "Look. I'm not like you, okay? I'm not like your family."

I don't understand what he's trying to say. "What do you mean, not like me? I'm sorry. I know I ask a lot of questions, I just—"

"It's not the questions, it's that you're not afraid of anything. I just, I'm not—" He checks his phone. "My mom should be back now. I'm just going to go home." He looks near tears. He quickly turns and runs toward his house, leaving me standing there on the sidewalk. *Not afraid of anything?* I was terrified just to *talk* to him! I thought we were actually becoming friends, but as I walk the rest of the way home I second-guess everything I've said, and can't figure out how I messed up.

Back at the bus, Dad is still somewhere inside the depths of the Victorian. The sounds of the screeching saw and my dad's radio station carries right through the window. Not much I can do about Leo right now. I don't even have his phone number to text him. I suddenly miss my mom so much my stomach feels hollow. In the bus, I flop down on my bed and page through the Annie Smith Peck book for a while, wondering if anyone ever accused her of not being afraid of anything. I mean, I *wish* I wasn't afraid of anything—like talking to other kids, that I'll never fit in at school, or trying to figure out what a whole year without Mom will be like.

I slam the book shut and get out my laptop instead. I start searching for "castles in New Jersey," but nothing comes up that seems like the one Leo was talking about. There are several on the East Coast, but they're all replicas built by dead, rich white men, or are actually resorts and not old at all. I find a few blog posts from the early 2000s with people talking about the legend, but no real information. I've been online for about an hour by the time Dad comes out of the house.

"Hey, Lindy-Lin. Shower time. Then grill. Then chat with Mom."

"Sounds good." We talk to Mom every Tuesday at six—it's a scheduled call she makes from a landline phone when she's on the mainland for food and supplies. My first thought is that I can't wait to tell her about Leo and Tinsley and the castle, but then I realize if she thinks nothing is wrong with her being gone, she might never want to come home. She has to think I'm still as miserable as I was last week when I was crying over having to make the fried plantains she usually makes.

Later, at dinner while we wait for Mom's call, I tell Dad a little bit about the castle. His face lights up like I knew it would. "Maybe we'll run into it on our moonlit hike on Saturday!"

I stuff potatoes in my mouth and nod even though I have no idea what Leo is going to do now. We didn't exactly leave off on friendly terms. Dad's phone vibrates on the table.

"That can't be your mother yet," he says. He checks it. "Oh, Leo's mom. That's odd."

I freeze as he answers.

"Hello, Lori, how are you this fine evening? . . . Oh, I'm sorry to hear that . . . Okay, of course I understand, no problem. Yes . . . You have a nice night too." He hangs up his phone and looks at me. "Leo doesn't want to come here the rest of the week, so his mom has him set up to spend the afternoons at his aunt's."

Leo was even more upset than I realized. "Did he say why?" I ask.

"She didn't give a reason." He looks at me as he helps himself to more salad. "Any ideas?"

I don't know how to explain to Dad that after running into the Sanders brothers, Leo seems to have decided he really does not like me. So I just shrug and say, "I have no idea."

We finish dinner without saying much more about it, and Mom calls at six on the dot, like always. "Hey, baby," she says. "How are you?" Her voice has this instant way of calming me down, like I'm being tucked into bed. But it also makes me sad, so it's a weird combo.

"I'm good, Mom. How're the turtles?" I know I sound short, but she doesn't seem to notice.

"So good. Oh my gosh, Lin, you can't even imagine! Today I was so lucky to witness the loggerheads. They're just beginning to nest, and it's simply incredible. You'd love it here so much."

Humph. *Yes, I would.* That's why we should have gone together, and then none of this awkwardness with Leo or the girls at school would have ever happened. "Maybe someday we could go again," I say, trying to sound upbeat but with a tiny bit of guilt trip on the side.

"It's definitely going on our family list. So how is everything at the bus? How's camp going? Have you met any friends yet?" She expertly changes the subject.

I lean on the counter and stare out the window at the purple house. "The bus is fine, and I decided to quit camp. Is that okay with you?"

She completely ignores my tone of voice. "Of course it's okay. You're an innovative girl. I'm sure you will come up with something to occupy yourself this summer."

I get up from the table and pace the bus. "Well, I did learn about a local legend today that was kind of cool. A hidden castle in the woods. I'm going to see if *Dad* will take me," I say, stressing the word *Dad*.

"That sounds like a wonderful idea!"

Not the response I was looking for. "Yeah, so I think I'll incorporate that into a movie about my first time on a solo adventure. Too bad you're going to miss it."

"It is too bad," Mom says. "I'd love to go with you. But we'll be back to our adventures soon. This is only for a year."

I can't take it anymore and plop down on a chair. "Do you have any idea how long one year feels to someone my age? It's worse than dog years!"

"It's going to go faster than you realize, especially once school starts," she says. "Just keep me posted on this castle!"

"There's no clue whatsoever to where it is."

"Well, *find* clues. Ask people in town, do a little investigating. I mean, you have all summer," Mom says in her always optimistic way. It makes me want to roll my eyes and hug her tight at the same time.

"Yeah," I say. Dad looks expectantly at me, so I tell her I love her and say goodbye and trade off the phone to him.

He holds it away from his ear and says to me, "You're going to tell me more about this castle," and winks before he gets back on with Mom. "Hey, how's my beautiful wife?" he says, and then drifts into the back of the bus.

I didn't even get to launch into all the other reasons Mom should not have left me behind. But she sounded like she's having such a good time, I feel bad doing that to her. She's been teaching and entertaining me for a long time. I suppose I can deal with one year without her. It just feels lonely without her here. Without her sleepy but cheery morning look over her coffee and how excited she always is to teach me the names of new plants and animals, how she shows me how to capture the best shots and edit videos. We always did everything together. I don't understand why suddenly turtles were more important.

I wander outside to the picnic table with the *Northeastern Foraging* book Mom bought me when they dropped the news we were moving to New Jersey. She always knows exactly what I like to read; I just wish it didn't feel like an apology for leaving. The sun has dropped a bit, but it's still really warm and muggy, reminding me a lot about our last flip, which was in Virginia, in the Shenandoah Valley. The area had similar forests to here, but I still learned a lot from Mom's book. Like in June you can find blueberries throughout the woods, especially across the river in Pennsylvania. And there are leafy plants in the mountains called ramps that smell like onions, but they can be really hard to find. In fact, there are all kinds of plants that you can eat, like dandelions and certain ferns, although by themselves they don't sound so delicious. And a lot of mushrooms too, but my parents say to leave them alone because it's too hard to identify the poisonous ones from the good ones.

Kind of like people, I think. My mind drifts to the mean girls in the bathroom and those angry Sanders boys. I wonder what made them like that. How do you become friends with people who seem so determined to . . . hurt you? And, honestly, how do you make friends even with those who aren't? Especially when there's a time limit on your friendship? I'm starting to wonder if it's actually worth it.

Crickets begin to chirp, and a dog barks somewhere in the distance. Every now and then a car passes. It's very peaceful. Until a high-pitched voice starts singing above it all.

"Popular, you're gonna be pop-u-lar . . ."

Tinsley Cooper's across the street twirling on the sidewalk and singing her heart out in a frilly blue dress and rainbow-colored combat boots. Part of me wants to duck under the table, like I'm watching something too personal to be part of. But clearly she has no problem being watched. So instead I wave. She waves back and bounces across the street to my yard like that's exactly what she was hoping I would do.

"Hey!" she says. "What's up?"

"Oh, nothing." For some reason, maybe because of the way Leo so quickly changed his mind about being friends, she's making me a little nervous too. She's totally out there, but she seems so confident. I feel like I'm right back at the beginning, where I'm afraid to say the wrong thing. "I . . . I was just saying hi."

"Oh." She grins. "Well, hi!"

"Who are you supposed to be now?"

"Glinda!"

"Like from *Wizard of Oz*?"

"*Wicked*. It's a Broadway show about the witches from Oz."

I'm kind of amazed by her. "Why do you dress up like different people all the time?"

"Why do you dress up like the same person all the time?" she shoots back, kind laughter in her voice.

I don't have any idea what to say to that, so I change the subject. "Can I ask you a question?"

She sits down at the table with me. "Sure! I love questions."

"Do you know what the story is with Leo Martin and the Sanders brothers?"

"Why?"

I tell her how our entire afternoon went. How we had such

a nice time together, went to Dilly's just like Dad suggested, talked about the castle, and everything was great. Until the Sanderses showed up. "Everything changed in an instant. And now he's not going to come here anymore."

Tinsley chews on her cheek a little bit. "I don't know him very well because he doesn't talk to many people at all. But I do know his mom is, like, crazy overprotective of him because he was sick all the time when he was little. He's never allowed to go on class trips unless his mom goes, stuff like that. Maybe he told her what happened, and she decided for him?"

"But why were they after him in the first place? He said he told on them about something."

Tinsley looks across the street. "I think that's Leo's story to tell, you know?"

"But he told you?"

Tinsley shakes her head. "I've heard rumors. I don't really know for sure." She scratches at a loose splinter on the table. "It's a small town. Things have a way of getting around fast, and getting scrambled up in the meantime."

I nod. "I have never lived in a small town."

"It's . . . mostly nice. But, hey, that castle Leo told you about? I, um . . . I *do* know something about that."

"You do?"

She leans in across the table. "Most people here think it's some goofy made-up story to try to get more tourists in town. No one takes it seriously anymore, and people haven't searched for it *forever*." She lowers her voice and sounds very mysterious. "But the truth is, it's a highly guarded ancient secret."

"Guarded by who?"

"The Freemasons."

"What's that?"

"It's a secret organization that's been around for, like, hundreds of years, all around the world." Tinsley moves her hands a lot when she talks. I get kind of swept up in her story immediately. "Most towns have a chapter, so their existence isn't secret or anything, but you can't be part of it unless you're brought in by another member. Ours here is one of the first in the US, so it's super old."

She totally has my attention. "Like a secret society? What do they do?"

"No one is sure, that's the thing. I think they were founded as stoneworkers and builders. And nowadays it's not really about that, it's more community programs and stuff. My dad is a member and I've overheard some conversations over the years. Not a lot, but enough to know that they know something about the castle and they definitely have information in their lodge about it."

"Can you ask him?"

Tinsley laughs. "No. Not a chance." She sits on the tabletop and swings her legs.

"Why? I don't understand."

"You can't ask a Freemason *anything*. It's just how the club works. I've tried, believe me. My dad doesn't even tell my mom what they do at their meetings. He gets dressed up; they wear these interesting apron things, lots of pins and patches." She pauses, like she's deciding whether to say any more. Then she adds, "When I was little he used to talk about the castle, how someday he'd take the time off to go search himself, but he never did. Somewhere along the line, he just stopped talking about it and now, well—"

"He can't because of his accident?"

Tinsley shakes her head. This is one of the strangest things I've ever heard. I can't imagine living here all my life, knowing there might be a castle in the hills and never at least *trying* to find it. I'm definitely jumping on the computer again as soon as Tinsley leaves and learning everything I can about Freemasons. "And you never went to go find it?"

Tinsley looks at me like it's the most ridiculous idea ever. "By myself? Up in the woods? Where *bears* live? Definitely not."

All I can think is if my mom was here right now, there's nothing in the world that would stop her from trying to find it. Not Freemasons, not bears, not even the fact that it might only be a legend. And now I feel like that's exactly what my mission is becoming: to find the castle this summer. It would make for an amazing movie, no question. And I think about all the good Mom does with her movies, to try to help make people appreciate the environment and, like she will with the turtles, learn about endangered species. Even her filming the show with Dad helps people appreciate making old homes new again—everything she does has a purpose.

Now it's my turn.

"I could show you the Mason lodge tomorrow," Tinsley says. "I mean, you can't go in it, but you could at least see where they hold their meetings."

"Yeah, that would be awesome! But won't you have to go to camp?"

Tinsley shrugs. "I don't think my mom will mind. Long as I tell them where I'm at. Do you have to go?"

"No, my parents said it was fine if I stopped as long as I had something to keep myself busy."

"Okay, cool," she says. "I'll come over in the morning." She hands me her phone. "Put your number in."

We trade phones, and just like that, I have my first contact in Newbridge.

"Thanks," I say. "I'll see you tomorrow."

She says goodbye and resumes singing on her way back across the street, leaving me smiling with my phone in my hand for a minute. And then I send her a smiley face just because.

She sends back an octopus.

I laugh and dash into the bus to look up everything about Freemasons that I can find, but Tinsley was right. There's not a lot to be uncovered online, other than they started as an actual stonemasons' club in England. They were men who built castles and cathedrals around Europe. Eventually it didn't matter if you were a stonemason or not, although they still only allowed men, which seems silly to me. The rumor, and mysterious part, is that they still guard a lot of secrets about ancient buildings, art, and history all over the world.

I suppose if anyone knows anything about an ancient castle in the woods, it's them. But Tinsley seemed pretty sure her dad would not be offering any information about it.

Which means, despite what Tinsley said about not being able to get in, tomorrow I have to find a way into that Freemason building.

The next morning, I wake up early, but Dad is already out in the house working. I stay in my little loft bed for a while, staring out the skylight window. I turn on the video camera and aim it up at the sky. Clouds cruise by, changing shape as they move, and a couple of vultures circle overhead. It looks like it's going to be a beautiful day. And my brain is full of strategies for breaking into a top secret building with a girl I just met who dresses up like different characters every day. A strange little twist, but certainly beats yesterday when I was hiding out in the bathroom stall feeling sorry for myself and taking pictures of scribbled walls. Now I have a plan and a purpose that's all mine.

I get up and get dressed, and make some oatmeal for breakfast. Tinsley knocks on the bus door at nine. She's wearing a black long-sleeve shirt that has a tie printed on it so it looks like she's wearing a suit jacket, shorts, tall black socks, and sneakers. I don't even have a chance to ask; she must be able to read the confusion in my face.

"*Umbrella Academy*," she says. "It's a show."

"Oh."

"You know, if you want to make movies, you should probably watch a little more TV. Ready?"

There she goes with really good points again, although Mom and I don't make those kinds of movies. More like little documentaries. "Yep. I just have to let my dad know we're leaving."

She follows me into the Victorian, where we follow the sound of a sander up the giant wraparound staircase and down a long hall past several rooms. At the end of the hall, Dad is working in the last bathroom, sanding a cabinet door.

He pushes his protective glasses up on the top of his head when we come into the doorway. "Hey, girls. Heading out for the day?"

"Yeah, we're going to go walk around town, if that's okay?" I ask. I know it is; I know he's thrilled that I'm going to be out and about.

"Go! Go see the world!" he says, and swats us away. "Text me if you need anything."

"Okay, thanks, Dad."

He smiles and turns the sander back on, sending clouds of dust everywhere. We make our way back into the fresh air and head toward town, which takes us right past Leo's house.

"Let's see if he's home," Tinsley said.

"He's probably already left for chess camp."

"It's early. Maybe he hasn't gone yet." She hops up the front steps and rings the doorbell. There's no answer, so she rings it again. Still nothing. "I'm going to check around back."

"Are you sure?" I ask, but then think if I'm going to sneak into some building in town, there's no reason to be afraid to jump a friend's fence. Even if he's a former friend. Tinsley climbs over without answering, and I follow. She knocks on the back door several times until we see a face peek out from under the curtain. It quickly drops.

"Leo Martin!" she shouts. "I see you in there!"

We wait a second, then hear the latch on the door. It opens, and Leo stands there looking half-angry, half-embarrassed. He's in sweatpants and a T-shirt with a dragon on it. His hair is a mess, but it looks kind of cute. He examines Tinsley's outfit. "Where did you even come from?" he asks, exasperated.

"My gram says a pepper patch," Tinsley says, as though that's a perfectly acceptable answer.

Leo has no response for her. He leans against the doorway and looks at me. "What do you want?"

"Come to town with us," Tinsley says. "I'm going to show Lin the Freemasons' lodge."

"Why?"

We explain the whole connection to the castle to him. He seems interested, but I can see the hesitation on his face and I'm sure it's because of what happened yesterday. "Town will probably be, um, empty since it's so early," I say.

"Yeah," Tinsley adds. "The only people up right now are people at work. It's summer break; everyone else is in bed!"

"Exactly where I was," he says. He looks at me again and sighs. "I told my mom I was sick. If she finds out I left the house, she'll seriously kill me. I can't risk it."

"Does she work in town?" I ask.

He shakes his head. "No, she's at the county hospital. She's a nurse."

"Then she'll never find out." I feel kind of bad trying to convince him to do something his mom doesn't want him to do, but I also really want him to come with us.

"She tracks me on my phone."

Tinsley rolls her head back. "Geez, this place is like Alcatraz or something. Just leave your phone here, then she'll think you're here."

Leo has a look on his face that makes it seem like this is the most excruciating decision he's ever had to make. After yesterday, I don't want him to feel that awful around me again. "Look, Leo," I say. "It's fine. If you don't feel good about coming, it's totally okay. We just wanted you to know we wanted you to come. But we can hang out another time, right?"

"Yeah," Tinsley says. "Like on Sunday! I'm having a pool party. Your mom will let you go to a pool party, at least?"

"I'm not sure. Because of Simon."

"Who's Simon?" I ask.

"My older brother," Tinsley says. "He used to hang out with the Sanders brothers. But he doesn't anymore, Leo. I already told you that. He's kind of a jerk to me sometimes, but he's not like those boys."

It's killing me that I don't know what happened to Leo, but he's not sharing, so I don't press it. It's better to let him be and not put pressure on him to break his mom's rules. "We'll catch up another time, okay? You can go back to bed."

We turn to go, but Leo calls after us from the doorway. He looks so torn. "Wait! I mean, this is stupid. You're right. I'm a prisoner in my own house. Give me five minutes." He closes the door. That was not the reaction I was expecting, but I'll take it. Maybe it means Leo isn't actually mad at me like I was fearing. Tinsley looks at me and says, "Yes!" and then we head around to the front yard and wait. Leo comes out the front door after a couple of minutes, changed and ready to go.

"So, what's the plan?" he asks as we walk down Third Street toward the Freemason building.

"We don't really have one—we're just hoping a door is open," I say.

"They supposedly protect the secrets of the universe, and you think the doors will be open?" he asks.

Tinsley laughs. "I don't think they have that much power, Leo. That's just in movies."

I step over a crack in the sidewalk. "We have to start somewhere."

When we reach the building, it's not what I expected. It's pretty much a boring three-story brick building like any other business in town. There's a little sign sticking out near the front door with a symbol that looks sort of like an *A* and a

V joined together, but is made of tools, which I recognize because my dad has them.

"Is that a square ruler?" I ask Tinsley.

"Yes, and some kind of drawing tool . . .'cause they were all builders originally, I guess."

"What's the *G* for?" Leo asks.

That's something I actually know. "Google said *geometry*."

"My dad says *God*," Tinsley answers with a shrug. "Should we see if the door is open?"

My hands start sweating. "Yes." The streets are empty, so we walk up and Tinsley tries the door.

"Locked." She looks at me, disappointed. "There's a door in the back lot, though. Let's try that."

We go around the side of the building, through a narrow passageway between the lodge and the next-door jewelry shop, stepping over broken beer bottles and cigarette butts. In the back parking lot, there are a few people gathered around, talking to a man dressed in a dark suit looking very official. We stay in the shadows.

"Great," Tinsley says.

"Who is he?" I ask.

"Mr. Sanders," Leo whispers. "The self-proclaimed king of Newbridge."

We're quiet for a few minutes, listening to their conversation. Only bits and pieces are clear, but they're talking about some kind of transaction. The only full sentence I hear is "Don't tell me you'll try, just get it done."

"Do you think they're going to go in?" Leo asks.

Tinsley says, "I thought the meetings were at night. And I don't think Mr. Sanders is a member, because my dad does *not* like him. But my dad hasn't been going for a while, since he was hurt, so I don't know." Something in her voice sounds a little angry. "Maybe Mr. Sanders has joined since."

"We have to wait anyway, so they don't see us. Let's cross over and we'll hide around the corner," I say. "Hopefully they'll leave soon."

We sit on the sidewalk curb on the street behind the building. Leo rolls acorns across the street between passing cars. A couple of people pass by and say hi to us, and every so often one of us runs around the corner to see if everyone's left.

Once they do, I shout, "Let's go!" We run across the gravel lot. Leo and Tinsley keep a lookout as I quickly try the door. But unfortunately it's also locked.

Leo shakes his head. "I knew it would never be this easy."

"We had to try," Tinsley says.

I stand back and study the building. There's a fire escape staircase on one side. "Think there's a door on the roof?" I ask Tinsley.

"I guess it's possible, but you can't go up there in the middle of the day."

"I wasn't thinking about going in the middle of the day," I say.

"You mean like sneak out tonight?" Tinsley asks. "Are you really that determined to get in there?"

I kick a stone across the lot. "I'm determined to go look for that castle. And we have no other leads on where to start."

"Well, how about I try to find out what night they all meet, and we wait until then to try to get in?" Tinsley suggests. It's a great idea, but I worry it will be weeks away. Still, probably better than climbing a fire escape onto the roof. We agree it's the best choice for now and start walking back to Tinsley's.

"Are you just going to come out and ask your dad about the meetings?" Leo asks. "I mean, if it's such a secretive club, will he even tell you anything?"

"No, I know he won't. But my mom keeps a very detailed, old-school calendar, so I'm pretty sure I can flip through and figure it out."

When we get back to Tinsley's, she tells us to wait in her tree house, which is actually a pretty cool little shack with colorful walls and a rug laid out inside. Someone, I assume Tinsley, has written quotes all over the panels, inspiring things about singing, dancing, performing, and little sketches of costumed characters.

"Wow," I say. "This is amazing."

Leo nods. "Kind of feels like I'm inside her head."

"Yeah," I say. We sit cross-legged on the floor. "What would this look like if we were inside *your* head?"

Leo thinks for a minute. "The Shire from *The Hobbit*."

I smile. "That's a good one."

He shrugs. "It's a peaceful place, as long as you stay in it."

"But Bilbo doesn't stay. He goes on an adventure."

"You've read that one too?" Leo asks, with more interest than I've seen on his face yet.

"Many times," I say. "I wonder if Tinsley would mind if I took a video of these walls."

"What would it look like in here if it was inside your mind?" Leo asks.

That's an easy one for me to answer. "Ice-capped mountains, meadows full of wildflowers, a huge roaring river of rapids and boulders across the whole inside. Maybe across the floor so it would be like you were sitting at the creek bed. Fish in the water, birds in the sky—"

"Wow. Sort of sounds like the rest of Middle-earth."

I laugh. "Actually, it's just some of my favorite parts of the United States."

"You really have seen everything, haven't you?" Leo asks.

"There's always more to see."

Leo looks at me for a short time without saying anything. I get the feeling he's trying to make sense of what I said, but I'm not sure why. And when he doesn't respond, I fiddle with my shoelaces, pretending they were loose and needed to be retied, until Tinsley returns.

She's carrying a glossy kitten calendar and a few sodas, which she tosses to us. She opens the calendar to January on the floor in front of us.

"Okay," she says as she scans each month. "Just have to figure out my mother's coding."

"Geez," Leo says. "You weren't kidding when you said this was detailed. Your family is busy!"

Tinsley shakes her head. "We're really not that busy. She has sort of a weird obsession of writing down every single thing she does. I mean, look: Who needs to record when they went to the post office? It's literally every minute of her days. She's addicted to Sharpies."

"There's a lot of doctor appointments," I say quietly.

All Tinsley says is "Yeah."

We flip through until we get to March, and there's a note on the last Monday written in yellow that says, "Lodge 8:00 P.M."

Tinsley taps it. "That's it! Not so secret after all." She flips to April, but there's no record of it.

"They don't meet every month?" I ask.

"Doesn't look like it."

"Or maybe the other meetings are so secret even your mom doesn't know," Leo says. Tinsley checks the other months, and there's nothing until the last Monday in June, two weeks away, although that one is crossed off.

"Whew," I say. "I was getting worried! Why is it crossed out, though?"

She shrugs. "I don't know, but can we wait that long?"

"I really wish we didn't have to," I say, wrapping my arms around my knees. We were just getting underway with something exciting, only to have to wait two weeks.

Tinsley stands up and reaches in her pocket. "I thought you might say that, so I grabbed these just in case. Ready?"

I have no idea what she's doing, but I hold out my hands. She drops a giant ring of keys right into them. "My dad's," she says. "One of them goes to the lodge."

"Are you sure?" I ask.

She sits down next to us. "Yep. We can go tonight. He'll never even know they're gone."

Leo looks a little unsure. To be fair, I'm a little unsure. But at least this way we're not climbing on a roof or technically breaking in. And I said I wanted an adventure, didn't I? There's one right here, right in front of me. I just have to claim it.

"All right," I say. "See you both back here tonight?"

"I'll be here!" Tinsley says.

Leo shakes his head but says, "I'll try."

One of the side effects of only ever being with adults is that you never really have to lie to them. It's a pretty cool thing to be treated like one of the grown-ups by your parents, honestly. I've never had to figure out how to get around anything because we always did everything together—there was nothing to get around! I think the biggest lie I ever told my mom was that I turned my light off before midnight when, really, I was under the covers reading. So telling my dad that I'm sleeping over Tinsley's—my first *real* sleepover—feels both extremely thrilling and extremely awful.

But Dad says he thinks it's "the bomb."

"Okay, Dad? Please. Let's not take it that far."

"I'm just excited for you!" He hugs me before I leave. "Your first sleepover!"

I guess it's not totally a lie. I *am* sleeping over, just not until after we sneak into a Freemason lodge.

At the tree house, Leo says he told his mom he's at my place, which she ended up being okay with. "I just told her I changed my mind about visiting you," he tells me, looking at the ground as he talks. "She loves your parents, so she's fine with it. She just wanted to make sure I was."

I just nod even though I really want to ask him if he told his mom what happened in town. I get the feeling he didn't.

All three of us are dressed completely in black—even Tinsley, although she added a black wig also, to cover up the hot-pink curls everyone would recognize. We prepare everything in the tree house. I call out the list, and they confirm.

"Flashlight?"

"Check."

"Notebook and pencil?"

"Check."

"Camera?"

"That's all you, and check."

"Phones are off?"

"Check."

"Time?"

"It's 9:36."

"All right. Let's roll!" I say, and tighten the strap on my camera. We could use our phones for photos, but I was afraid we'd end up dropping one, which could mean making too much noise and getting caught, or even worse, losing a phone and leaving it behind. Plus, I plan on filming some of the night for the movie, so my camera will be enough and all phones will stay in pockets. Except for Leo's, which we hid in the Victorian in case his mom feels the need to look up where he is.

"You think of everything," Leo says. "Have you been involved in heists prior to this one?"

"Ha. No. And it's not a heist. We're not taking anything from the lodge; we won't even move anything. It's like when you go camping in a state park: Leave no trace. We can just take pictures and video of anything we think might be important for finding the castle."

"Won't it take forever to get photos back with that old camera?"

I shake my head. "It's not that old. It's digital, so I can plug it right into my laptop and pull them up on the screen. It'll be fine."

We climb out of the tree house and start making our way to town by sticking to the sidewalks and alleys on less traveled roads. Staying out of the glow of streetlights, we run from shadow to shadow. Newbridge is very quiet at night. A dog barks somewhere in the distance, but other than that the crunching of gravel under our feet and crickets chirping are the only sounds. When a car comes, we duck until it's passed us. Last thing we need is to run into a parent, or worse, the Sanderses. Fortunately we reach the lodge with no problem. The next challenge is going through the entire ring of keys before someone sees us.

"Let's try at the back door," I say. "Less chance of someone walking by. I'll keep an eye out here; Leo, you go out to the corner, okay? And Tinsley will try the keys."

Everyone nods and takes their posts. Leo seems hesitant to

go out to the curb, but he does, and crouches in shadows. I scan the parking lot and the passageway between buildings as Tinsley tries key after key. Totally quiet, no people anywhere.

"Why does your dad have so many keys?"

"No idea," she says. "But one has to be for here."

A car passes Leo but keeps going. There are some voices in the distance, but I don't see anyone. They must be coming from around the front, probably people passing by the lodge.

"Hurry," I whisper.

Finally, the doorknob turns. Tinsley holds back a squeal, and I grab her shoulders out of excitement. I'm unable to stop grinning as I wave to Leo, and he runs back and slips inside the dark building with us. I turn on the video camera and let it record without aiming it, like an action camera, but retro. It's really too dark to see anything, but it will still make some cool footage for my movie later.

Inside, it's completely black except for a red exit light over the door. It's dank and smells a little bit like an old refrigerator. I pull the flashlight out of my bag and light up the space, and Tinsley and Leo do the same. We're in a small foyer that has tons of framed photographs on the walls. All seem to be groups of men from decades and decades of membership in the club. When I pass the light over them, I can see that the oldest date, on a brown wrinkled photo, is 1888.

"Wow, this *has* been around for a long time," I whisper. "And every single member really is a man. I wonder why?"

"Just the way it is," Tinsley says.

"Well, that's dumb." I push through a second set of double doors that aren't locked, and we make our way into the main hall. There are more photos on the walls, more men dressed in colorful sashes or aprons. In some, they seem to be performing rituals or initiations. It all definitely seems formal and secretive, but at the same time, really cool. "They don't seem to be doing anything women can't do."

"I don't know if it's a true rule," Tinsley says. "Just only men seem to join. My dad said it's not the kind of club girls would like."

Mom has told me about all kinds of clubs that used to be like that, only for men. But over the years people started making changes because they realized they were missing out on other people's ideas. She said, "No matter what you want to do in life, Lin, being a girl shouldn't stop you, thanks to all the work women ahead of us have done." I honestly kind of rolled my eyes on the inside when she'd say stuff like that, but now I see it. She was totally right. If the Freemasons truly value historical secrets, you'd think they'd get as many people involved as possible to preserve them.

"How would he know girls wouldn't like it if none are in it?" I ask Tinsley.

"Good question!"

"Check this out!" Leo says. He holds the door so Tinsley and I can go inside what turns out to be a huge and very fancy auditorium, similar to a church, or like the inside of an ancient cathedral, only smaller. It has super-high ceilings, with ornate columns and long bench seats, and enormous paintings on the walls that are so big our flashlights can't even light up the entire thing. Busts and sculptures are lined up around the walls. I would never have had any idea something so fancy was inside this plain brick building.

"It's like a museum of natural history or something in here!" I say. My voice booms in the room, making me duck a bit. "Oops."

"Why do they have all this stuff?" Leo asks. He walks around the room slowly, shining his light on every shelf, box, and wall hanging he can find.

"I guess it's like Lin said—it's like a museum; they keep things safe. Just not open to the public." Tinsley shines her light on a jeweled headdress in a glass box. "So, what do you think we should be looking for? This whole place is a treasure chest."

"I have no idea," I say. "It's a random collection of art and artifacts." How are we supposed to know where to start? This could take days!

Leo stands beneath a giant colorful tapestry hanging in the back of the room, right in the center above the doors we came through. His flashlight only exposes a small section. "If I had any guess, knowing the legend, this would be one of the clues."

Tinsley and I walk over and shine our lights on the tapestry. Together, we brighten up most of it. It's an image of a round table with colorful shields and swords arranged in a circle. Each shield has a different symbol, and every sword has a single letter on the hilt. Except for one at the top, which has two letters.

"King Arthur's Round Table," Leo says.

"How do you know?" Tinsley asks.

Leo points with his light. "Twelve seats. The letters on the top sword are *AP*—"

"Arthur Pendragon," I say.

Leo looks at me with so much admiration it makes my stomach flutter. "Yes," he says. "King Arthur's real name."

"So the rest of those letters must stand for each knight's name?"

"Yeah, probably. But look at the image in the middle."

We all focus our lights in the center. There are symbols that look like a language but don't make any sense to us. I aim the video at the tapestry and take a few still shots. It's so dark, though, this old camera can't pick up all the detail. But maybe a smartphone can.

Even though it's breaking our rules, I reach for my phone, but something suddenly crashes out in the hall and all three of us grab for one another. My phone falls to the floor. We crouch, huddle together, and turn off our lights. We wait for a few minutes, but hear nothing besides our own breathing. In the dark, I bend lower and feel around for the phone. Finally, my fingers find it.

"Maybe something just fell off a wall out there?" Leo whispers. "Lin, did you get photos?"

"Not yet. I need to use my phone's flash," I say. "It's brighter."

"Hurry," Tinsley says. "Take the picture so we can get out of here!"

I take several, including some close-ups of the center of the tapestry, and then we make our way back into the hall. Sure enough, there's a photo frame that seems to have fallen off the wall, now lying facedown on the ground. I sigh. "That's all it was."

"Should we hang it back up?" Tinsley asks.

"Might as well," I say.

Tinsley walks over to the frame, turns it around, and brings it back to us. "Look at this."

It's a photo of two men standing on top of a stony ridge with hiking poles. On either side of them is a pair of boulders stacked in a way that could only have been done by people. And across the bottom is handwritten: *Holiday and Harper, Pen's Overlook, Kittatinny Mountain, 1966*.

"Holiday?" Tinsley says. "That must be Mr. Holiday from the hardware store."

"And Pen's Overlook," Leo adds, and taps the photo. "Like Pendragon!"

Before I can say anything, a shadowy figure emerges down the hall. It's too dark to make out any features.

"I thought I heard something," a female-sounding voice says. "How did you three get in here?"

She doesn't sound angry, only curious, but we can't take

our chances. "Let's get out of here!" I shout, and start pushing both Tinsley and Leo in the opposite direction of the voice.

In the rush toward the door, Tinsley drops the photo and the glass shatters. So much for not leaving a trace. We run back down the hall the way we came in. We hold on to one another's shirts, each of us pushing the other out into the night, half laughing, half screaming the entire time. We slip out and the door slams behind us. None of us stop to wait and see if the person follows, we just keep running for our lives. I clutch the camera against my middle, and we run until we are several blocks away and completely out of breath, still laughing. It's funny how you can laugh even when you're scared.

"Oh my god, that was so close," Tinsley says, gasping.

"I know! I thought we were dead!" I say. I don't even realize how far behind Leo is until he tells us to wait up.

"Hang . . . on," Leo says, pressing against his side. "I can't . . . run anymore."

"You okay?" I stop and wait for him to catch up.

"Yeah," he says. "Just a stitch in my side. You two took off like cheetahs! I have shorter legs!"

We all crack up, but walk slower now. "You should have seen your face, Leo," Tinsley teases, and makes an open-mouthed, wide-eyed terrified look.

"Shut up," he says, still catching his breath. "Like you should talk. We were all freaked out."

I look back every so often, but it seems we got away clean. "That was amazing," I say, finally catching my breath. I feel like we did get away with a heist, though in reality, we didn't do anything that terrible other than snoop around and take some pictures. I can't wait to get back and look through everything more closely. But now I almost wish I'd shone my flashlight on that person's face to see who it was.

"Didn't that sound like a woman's voice to you?" I ask.

"Yes," both Tinsley and Leo say.

"But I thought you said the club was only for men?"

"Maybe I was wrong," Tinsley says.

"Maybe," I say. But there was something odd about it all. Why was she there when there wasn't a meeting? In the dark. Apparently knocking things off the wall. It didn't add up.

"Uh. Guys?" Tinsley stops walking. She pats her pockets down.

"What is it?" I ask.

She looks at me with wide eyes and then covers them like she can't bear to see my reaction. "I think I left the keys in the door."

7

I check my phone. It's ten thirty. No texts from Dad, so that's good. He's probably sound asleep and dreaming of fancy circular saws with diamond teeth. But can we actually risk going back to the scene of the crime? I kind of want to see who that woman was, but I don't want us to get in trouble. It's not worth it. This was not in my plan.

"It's fine," Tinsley says. "You two go home. I don't want you to get in trouble for my stupid mistake. I'll go grab them, if they're still there." She starts walking.

"No way you're going alone," I say. "We're in this together."

"It's okay," Tinsley says as she's backing away. "I'll be right back. I can be sneaky and I'm fast, you'll see!" She dashes off before I even have a chance to tell her to wait.

"Shoot," I say. "Why'd she do that?"

"I guess she felt bad," Leo says.

I look down the road in the direction she went, and then at Leo. He paces on the curb, balancing as he walks, and I keep checking my phone. A big delivery truck goes by, and we both hide behind a tree. It feels like too much time has passed since Tinsley left. "This is a bad idea. I shouldn't have let her go alone."

Leo looks how I feel: guilty.

"It's fine. You wait here," I tell him. "Or actually, maybe head home so you don't risk getting caught. I'll go check on her."

"Are you sure we should all split up?"

"I'm sure. There's no reason for you to get in trouble. Wait for us back at the bus." I start to go, but then stop. "Wait. Can you take the camera?"

He takes it, and I start jogging back toward town. There's a sinking feeling in my gut, almost like I ate something bad and it's sitting in the pit of my stomach. Hopefully Tinsley hasn't been caught. I'll feel terrible.

When I turn the corner, Tinsley is already heading my way. Her shoulders droop a bit. "They were gone," she says when we reach each other.

"Oh no," I say. "That lady?"

"I guess?" She shrugs. "My dad is going to flip out."

"Does he use those keys a lot?"

"Not every day or anything, but they are the keys to just about everything around the house." She sounds like she might cry, but she keeps it together. "As soon as Simon has to go out in the shed for the lawn mower, they're going to know."

"Well, I mean. He won't know you took them. Maybe he'll just think he misplaced them. Or that Simon left them in the shed."

Tinsley doesn't say anything for a while. "Yeah."

"Are you all right?" I ask.

"Yeah. It's just, with my dad still in bed and all, and then he'll think his keys are missing?" She sighs. "I feel bad that this will worry him."

I have to make this right. "We'll find them. I'll go back in the morning and look harder."

"Thanks, Lin, but they're definitely not there. I'm just going to head home, okay? I'll stop by tomorrow." She waves and disappears into her side yard. I have the same feeling as when Leo walked away from me: like I messed up big time. Real friendship seems to be just out of my reach all the time, and I don't know how to make it any different. I either say the wrong thing or do the wrong thing. I stand on the sidewalk for a couple of minutes debating on texting her and apologizing. I send a castle emoji instead.

Back at the Victorian, I find Leo inside sitting on the steps with only his phone for light. "This place is creepy. Do you know it makes creaky and dripping noises constantly?"

"Yeah," I say, and sit next to him on the steps, sighing. "Tinsley went home for the night. She couldn't find the keys."

"Oh. Then what are we going to do?"

"I'm going to have to think about it."

Leo stands up. "All right, well, I've got to get back home. My mom texted to be back by eleven, so I've got just enough time."

"Text me when you get in." I hand him my phone the way

Tinsley did, and just as I hoped, he types in his number. I can't help but smile. Collecting contacts is a new thing for me.

"I will." He gives my phone back, waves, and leaves out the front door. I stay on the steps for a few minutes. Leo wasn't kidding about noises. Creak. Drip. Groan.

Not sticking around for ghosts, I head back to the bus, and lie down in bed with my phone. The photos came out pretty good, and I zoom in to try to get a good look at the symbols. I do a lot of searching online, but nothing turns up. I think the best way for me to figure any of this out is going to be to try the library.

Even though we don't stay in one place very long, Mom and I have found that libraries usually give us temporary cards. You can't buy too many books when you live in a bus! A lot of the time when we do buy books, we'll even end up donating a bunch to the library's book sale before we head to a new place. Mom says it's a nice way to return the favor. Hopefully Newbridge Library will be willing to give me a card, but if not, I can just read some books on local legends and history while I'm there.

Eventually I tuck the phone under my pillow and fall asleep for hours, only waking up when Dad starts brewing coffee.

"Good morning, Lindy-Lin," he says when I open my curtain. "You came back early."

Light pours through the skylight over me, causing me to squint. I stretch and yawn. "Tinsley had to help her mom with something," I say, hoping it sounds true enough.

"Plans for the day?" he asks.

"I think I'm going to go check out the library."

Dad slides in at the table and lets the steam of his coffee warm his face. He closes his eyes and breathes in. "That sounds like an excellent idea. I'm surprised you hadn't done that weeks ago."

"Yeah." I roll on my side so I can see him better. "Well, it's different now."

"What's different?" He smiles, and I know he's waiting for me to tell him he was right: that making friends would be a game changer.

"Just is. I can't depend on Mom anymore; you work sixteen hours a day; so . . ."

Dad puts his mug down with a clunk, I think louder than he meant. "Hey, easy."

"Sorry," I say. And I am, but maybe not entirely, since none of this was my choice. "I just mean, you were right, okay? I admit it. I needed to try harder to make friends." Even though I'm not entirely convinced I've done a great job of that. "But I also realize now that I have to depend on myself."

He gets up from the table, comes over to me, and kisses my forehead. "You can always depend on us. You just can't always expect us to be your entertainment. Things are changing around here, and they will probably continue to. But we're a family, and we will always depend on one another."

I don't really like how he mentioned things would continue

to change. I guess I already realized that. Who's to say that Mom won't end up doing something like this again, plus us staying in one town for over a year—something we've never done before—and Dad even pausing the show. It's like we're all hitting the reset button this summer.

"All right, sweetheart. I'm heading out into the purple monster. Enjoy the library. And be careful crossing the streets."

"Dad. Seriously?"

He pinches my nose. "I'm always serious." And then he crosses his eyes and sticks out his tongue.

"Never do that again," I say, throwing the sheet back over my face.

He makes a funny villainous laugh as he leaves the bus, and I have to suppress a giggle so he doesn't hear me. I send a text to Leo and Tinsley that I'm going to the library and to meet me later if they want. Then I get dressed, grab an apple and my bike, and head to town.

I'm beginning to really like wandering around, seeing the same neighbors out every day, people watering gardens or walking their dog. I thought stuff like that would get old fast, but there's actually something a little comforting about it. It's different from waking up to see Mom's and Dad's faces every morning, but it's starting to feel like home in a new way.

I turn down Union Street and park my bike in the rack outside the library. It's an old stone building with tall windows in front, and sort of looks ancient on the outside, but inside is very modern and clean. It's two stories of shelves and work space, and I make my way through to the main desk.

A young man looks up at me. "Hi, how can I help you?"

"Two things," I say. "I'd like to get a card, and I also wanted to know if you had any books on Freemasons, King Arthur, and local legends?"

He looks impressed. "That's quite a list. And I can help you with all of it." He takes all my information for the card and then realizes who I am. "Oh, you're that family that moved in to flip that old purple place!"

"Yep, that's us." I hope he doesn't want to know everything about my famous parents right now, because I really don't have the time.

He hands me my new library card. "My name is Jackson—nice to meet you."

"Thanks." I slip my new card in my back pocket.

He stands up from the desk. "Follow me. I'm going to lead you to someone who can help you."

We walk through the library and up to the top floor where Jackson introduces me to an older woman named Darla. "Lin here is from the famous Moser family!"

Darla says nothing.

"Anyway, she would like some help with local information, and I thought you might be able to answer some of her questions." Jackson smiles at me and says, "Good luck!" the same way you say good luck to someone who's about to jump off a roof to see if they can fly. And then he leaves to get back to the desk.

Darla looks skeptical. "What do you want to know?"

"I was hoping to find some books about Freemasons, King Arthur, and some local history."

She smirks at me. "You're going to go look for Pen's Castle?"

"I—"

"Don't bother." She stands up and starts walking away. I'm not sure if I'm supposed to follow her until she turns and says, "Well, do you want books or not?"

I keep pace with her as she leads me to a small room off in a corner. "Why don't bother?" I ask. "Do you know anything about it?"

"I only know two things: It's dangerous up there, and plenty of people have tried to find it well before you were born and never did. So there's no reason to believe you will, or that it exists at all." She points to a shelf. "Start there. Articles from the fifties and sixties, the last time the castle was hot news. You won't find any of that on the internets." She points to another shelf. "Books by local authors. Should be enough to get you started. Don't make a mess." Then she leaves the room and closes the door.

Okay, then, nice to meet you too. I pull one of the newspapers from the files. Each is in a protective plastic cover, so I carefully pull it out and open it on the large table in the middle of the room. I wonder why these wouldn't be online, but I guess she's right, considering every search I tried before I didn't find anything. I page through several of the newspapers, and there are a few short articles about people coming to town to search for the infamous "Castle in the Clouds," but there's nothing all that helpful.

The local authors' book section is also small. *Weird Newbridge*, *The Legend of the Quarry*, and *Secrets of New Jersey* seem the most likely to have something interesting. But I spend at least an hour and again find nothing other than people talking about the legend, which is not much more than what Leo and Tinsley already told me. What I really need is a clue about where to start looking.

I suddenly get a text from Tinsley: *We're here! Where are you?*

I explain where the little room is, and she comes through the door about thirty seconds later. Dressed like a pilot. Leo comes in after her with his hands raised like he has no explanation for her. "Don't look at me," he says.

"Amelia Earhart," Tinsley says, and waves her hand as if wearing a pilot jumpsuit and aviators to the library is expected. "So, have you found anything good yet?"

"Not really." I show them everything I've read so far, and the three of us continue to skim through newspapers for a little bit.

"The librarian said these shelves were what I needed," I say, placing my hands on the papers. "But, Tinsley, maybe you can check that side? And Leo the ones in the back?"

"Yeah, maybe things get mixed up," Leo says. "Worth looking around a little bit."

"Why do they keep all of this?" Tinsley asks as she blows dust off a pile of magazines. "Isn't it all online now? When I did my history project this year, our teacher showed us how to search online archives."

"I don't know. The lady said these weren't, but not sure about the rest of the room."

Tinsley starts searching her phone for something. "I just want to see if . . . yes, here, look. This is the website we used." She shows us her phone and the image of the same paper that's spread out on the table.

"Oh," I say. "That's weird. I didn't double-check."

"But wait." She scrolls through for a minute, compares her phone to the paper a few times, and then nods. "Wow. This *is* weird."

"What?" Leo asks.

"The librarian wasn't lying. Every article is viewable except that one," she says, tapping the little blurb about a hiking team that came to town in 1956.

"Try another!" I say, and then open my phone also. "I'll look too."

We spend about a half hour searching as many of the online newspapers as we can. And sure enough, every paper is scanned online, but every single article about the castle or town is blurred out.

"It's a cover-up," Tinsley says. "Has to be."

"But why?" I ask. "And who could pull that off?"

Leo looks at Tinsley. "The Freemasons? Didn't you say they were a worldwide group?"

I shiver. What could possibly be so important about the castle, if it truly exists, that they'd erase any proof of its existence, or even proof of others just searching for it? "This is weird, guys."

"Very," Tinsley says. "But then again, if it *is* the Freemasons, they must have a good reason. I mean, I don't think my dad would be part of something . . . bad."

"Like it truly is part of King Arthur's legend?" I ask. Tinsley shrugs but seems like she's worried about what the truth is. "It might have been done way before your dad was even part of the group," I tell her. "Right? We don't know how much he knows. But maybe you could try asking him again?"

"Maybe," Tinsley says. "But I think he likes keeping it a mystery. Something just for him, you know?"

I totally know.

I take photos of the articles just so we have them. Nothing seems important now, but maybe something will later. Tinsley helps me fold all the papers back up and get them in their covers to file. Leo wanders around the shelves and comes back with a very old, worn book with a cover that looks like it was once colorful, but is now pretty tattered.

"Check this out," he says, holding it up. The title isn't in English. *Historia Regum Britanniae.*

"What does that mean?" Tinsley asks.

Leo looks a little hesitant.

"I get the feeling Leo is about to nerd out big time right now," Tinsley says to me. "I'm kidding, Leo. What is it?"

"It's the history of the kings of Britain. One of the first books that mentions King Arthur, and basically where the legend all started." He opens it up and shows me. "Unfortunately, it's all in Latin. And I might be a nerd, but I'm not that big of a nerd. I have no idea what it says."

I take the book and carefully look through. There are a ton of illustrations. "Maybe we don't need to know what it says. Maybe we just need these." I tap on a page that looks very much like the style of the tapestry at the Freemason building.

"No way," Tinsley says. "Look at all those symbols."

I take a quick picture of the page, and suddenly the door swings open. For some reason my reaction is to hide the book behind my back. But it's just Darla. "All right, kids. Archive room time is up."

"There's a time limit?" I ask.

"Yeah." Darla looks like she's thinking up an answer. "At least on Thursdays."

We glance at one another. "Can I take out any of the books in here?" I ask.

Darla shakes her head. "All reference room material stays in the reference room."

I can tell she's not going to change her mind, so I say, "Okay, I just have a couple notes to take down."

Darla nods and leaves.

“There’s no time limit,” Leo says. “She totally made that up right now.”

“Probably just doesn’t want us in here, afraid we might ruin things,” Tinsley says. “But we’re all good, right?”

“Yeah,” I say, looking at the book again. “But first I need to take a bunch of pictures of this.”

8

Once we're out of the library, Tinsley asks if we want to hang out at her tree house and compare the photos of the tapestry to the book.

"Yes, definitely," I say. "But first, I want to make one other stop and talk to Mr. Holiday about that photo at the lodge. See if it's really him in the picture."

"Good idea," Leo says. "Let's do that and then go eat lunch."

"Aren't you worried about your mom finding out?" I ask.

"No." He balances on the curb as we walk. "I mean, I left my phone at home just in case she tracks me, but yeah. I'm trying not to care *too* much."

"She just worries about you. Moms do that," Tinsley says.

"Mine does it too much," Leo says.

"Well, mine moved to a deserted island for a year, so she's clearly not worried," I say, but I don't mention that if she was home I'm pretty sure she would never track me on my phone, and she'd definitely let me walk to town.

"Your mom is the coolest mom on the planet, Lin," Tinsley

says. "World traveler, filmmaker. I mean, come on, I want to be her when I grow up." Before I can say, *Yeah, me too*, Tinsley puts her aviators on and holds out her arms and sings, "Off we go, into the wild blue yonder, climbing high into the sky."

Leo turns bright red. "You are so embarrassing." But he's laughing as he says it. Tinsley swoops around him in a big circle.

"People are going to think there's something wrong with you," he says.

"Live a little, Leo Martin!" she says. "Who cares what people think!" And she goes right on singing and twirling, which is definitely braver than I could be.

We walk a couple of blocks to Holiday Hardware (well, Tinsley flies), and once inside, it smells a lot like the house Dad's working on: sawdust and coffee and a little bit of sweat.

Mr. Holiday is at the counter reading a newspaper. He's a big man with a very round and kind face and a bushy gray beard. He closes the paper when we approach. "Why, hello there. What can I do for you?"

"Hi, Mr. Holiday," I say. "My name is Melinda Moser, and my dad—"

"I know exactly who your father is, young lady. It's nice to finally meet you. Welcome to Newbridge." He smiles. "And hello, son. Leonardo, right?"

Leo nods.

Mr. Holiday looks at Tinsley. "And you must be Amelia?"

She grins the biggest grin ever.

He looks back to me. "Your dad need something else for the house? He was just in here the other day picking up quite a haul."

I fold my hands on the counter. "No, sir. It was recently brought to our attention that you have maybe gone to look for the Castle in the Clouds."

Mr. Holiday laughs. "Brought to your attention, huh?"

I don't want to give away that we were sneaking around the lodge, so I skip over the photo and say, "Yes, and if it's true, we're curious what you know about it."

Just then the bell on the door rings, and a few other people come in—a young couple and a woman around my parents' age who looks like she's dressed to go hiking.

"Good morning. If I can be of help, let me know!" Mr. Holiday calls out to them. The couple nod and keep walking, but the woman walks up to the counter. We all take a step back to give her some room so she can ask him her question. She has a long blond ponytail and is wearing hiking boots and cargo pants with a million pockets—which I'm actually really jealous of. You could carry everything in those pockets.

"Do you copy keys here?" she asks.

"Yes, ma'am, I sure do." He looks at us. "I'll be right with you three." And then he walks the woman to another counter where the machine is. She glances at us and then follows him over.

I grab Leo's and Tinsley's arms and pull them into an aisle with me. I write a note on my phone instead of talking and lift it up to show them.

That woman. I recognize her voice!

They both nod, and we watch her. She presents Mr. Holiday with a single key, rather than a whole ring of them like I think we were all expecting. While he cuts the key, she looks back at us. We duck back into the aisle and press our backs against the shelves with boxes of screws and nails, knocking several to the floor. I cringe as little nails go everywhere.

"Don't you kids go and make a mess of my shop, now!" Mr. Holiday shouts from the key machine.

"Sorry, sir!" I shout back. "It was an accident! We're cleaning it all up!"

"That has to be the lady from the lodge. Do you recognize her? Is she from here?" I whisper to Leo and Tinsley as we scoop up handfuls of nails.

"I've never seen her before," Tinsley whispers. Leo shakes his head no. We wait until they return to the checkout counter. Mr. Holiday rings her up and says goodbye and then she's gone. *Maybe it's nothing,* I think. Lots of people get copies of keys. And I could be mistaken about her voice. We come out of hiding and back up to the counter.

Mr. Holiday leans on his elbows on the counter. "You got all those nails picked up?"

"Yes, sir." I place a broken box on the counter. "I'm sorry about this one."

"Nothing a little tape can't fix," he says, and puts the box under the counter. "So the famous castle, huh? What makes you think I know anything about it?"

I'm not sure if we should mention the photo in the lodge, so I say, "Just heard a rumor that you tried to find it when you were younger."

He nods but stays quiet for a long time, which makes me wonder if he's going to say anything at all. Finally he leans all the way across his counter toward us and says gravely, "You know what they say about rumors, don't you?"

I shake my head, afraid I've somehow completely offended him.

He leans in closer and whispers, "Sometimes rumors are true." After a long pause, he starts laughing.

I can feel Leo and Tinsley looking at me, waiting for me to be the one to respond. "So . . . you did try?"

Suddenly he stands up and smacks the counter. "I sure did. I tried half a dozen times back in the day. Everybody did back then. It's a lost cause."

"Oh."

He sighs. "Fun thing to daydream about, though. When I was about your age, the legend went through sort of a revival, you could say. Happens a lot with stories like that—aliens, the Loch Ness Monster, Bigfoot—they come and go with intensity over the years. Back in the fifties people came out here to Newbridge a lot more trying to find it. By then the Appalachian Trail was only about thirty or forty years old, so that brought a lot more curious hikers. Before then, people were just blindly searching the woods."

"But the trail wasn't built to find the castle?" I ask.

"No, the trail has been here much longer, but it helped get people up the mountain when it was opened as a public park. Then it got extended down here to town. And so we were always full of folks coming in from all over. I grew up on that story like Santa Claus. We all *wanted* it to be true, but figured it probably wasn't."

"But you went looking anyway?" Leo asks.

"Yep. First time I was fourteen. It was me, my brother, and a few friends. Nothing was going to keep us from hiking up there and trying to find out for ourselves if it truly existed. The last time was in my twenties with a buddy from high school. I think we were close that time. If there's anything truly there, we were definitely close."

"Why do you say that?"

Mr. Holiday looks at me for a minute, almost like he's wondering if he can trust me with this information. "There are carvings up there. At Pen's Overlook. In the rocks. Old symbols. Might just be from someone messing around, but in my young mind they were directions of some sort. But they never made any sense to me."

Pen's Overlook was where the photo was taken that we saw in the lodge, so it seems Mr. Holiday is telling the truth so far. "And after that you never went again?"

"A young man has to grow up. I got married, started a business. Ain't got time for hiking!"

Tinsley flashes her brilliant smile. "Can you tell us how to find the symbols at least?" she asks.

"I can, but you have to promise me you're going with a grown-up. It's treacherous up there. It might not seem terribly high, but it's mighty rocky, and those rocks can shift at a moment's notice. I can't stand to think you three little ones would be up there alone."

I stiffen at what feels like an insult. Mr. Holiday has no idea how much hiking Mom and I have done, but launching into the fact that we've visited tons of state and national parks just for that reason would be rude. Besides, I know he means well. "Of course not. My dad is going to take us this weekend."

"Takes a child's imagination to be motivated, and an adult's strength to actually climb up there. I suppose you'll all be a good team." He stands up straight, folds his newspaper, and tucks it under the counter. "As far as I know, people gave up looking a long time ago, so maybe you'll start a whole new trend!"

He gets out a blank piece of scrap paper and draws a little map on it. He spins it around for us to see as he explains it.

"Straight up the public trail for five miles until you come to a huge grove of rhododendrons. Look 'em up if you don't know what they are."

"I know what they are," I say. "Huge purple flowers, broad-leaved evergreen bush . . . " I trail off and then look at Leo and Tinsley for their reaction. But they don't seem to care. They don't even look at me, just wait for Mr. Holiday to continue.

"That's where you leave the public trail," he says. "And head north to the rock scramble, which will take you over the first of three rocky ridges. Continue north, but after the second ridge, look for a giant boulder stacked on top of another giant boulder. We call that Pen's Overlook."

"Each boulder is bigger than a car, and they sit in the middle of nothing, like a giant plucked 'em off the ridge and set them down in the middle of the woods. You can't miss it. Etched on the rock, you'll see symbols that look something like this." He draws a few wavy and geometric symbols on the back. "Best my memory is, anyway. After that, your guess is as good as mine, 'cause we never did figure out what those symbols meant."

I place my hand on the little map and thank him. It feels like gold or silver under my fingertips. It must be protected at all costs. "Thank you so much, Mr. Holiday. I just have one more question."

"You're welcome. And shoot!"

"Are you a Freemason?"

Mr. Holiday looks at me curiously at first, and then shakes his head. "No, no, I'm not, but I've had a few friends involved. I never had much interest. Why?"

"Just curious," I say. The other guy in that photo with Mr. Holiday must be a member and a friend of his.

Mr. Holiday taps the counter to get my attention. "You know, it sure would be amazing for that legend to be true. And seems fitting that the famous Mosers might be the ones to find it." He winks at us, and we all say goodbye. Then we head back out into the warm afternoon.

"We have to laminate this or something," I say as I study the directions. "Make sure it never gets torn or wet. This map is priceless."

"Take a picture of it too," Leo says. "Just in case."

"Good idea." I open my phone camera and quickly take a photo of the paper. I can't believe our luck with Mr. Holiday. For the first time it really feels real. The castle is up there, I know it. Now it's up to me to find it.

I turn on the video camera and aim it at Leo and Tinsley. Leo teases by holding up a hand to block his face, but Tinsley instantly throws her arms out dramatically and sings, "We are the champions!"

Leo groans, but I actually know this song, and after I get a little more footage of Tinsley's free show, I hum along with her. I even find myself skipping alongside her a little bit as we make our way home for lunch. My face hurts from grinning so much. Who knows, maybe she'll even get me to dress up?

"Hey, it's the Three Musketeers," Dad says when he sees us come into the yard, which kills my vibe a little bit since that's *my* name for our family. He has two wooden supports set up to form a table so that he can sand a door on it. But I don't say anything about the Musketeer thing because he also has an expression on his face that means bad news.

"What is it?" I ask. I know his faces; there's no sense in dragging out whatever it is he has to tell me. "Mom's okay, right?"

"Oh gosh, yes, Lin. She's completely fine." He sets down the tools and dusts off his hands. "She did call, though. She ran into some issues with equipment not working, and she needs me to head out to the storage unit for a few things. I can't do it until Saturday, which is going to mess up our plans."

"Okay. So can't we hike after?"

"That unit is an hour away, and I'm going to have to pull everything out. It's just a mess, hon. I think we're going to have to postpone our hike until next weekend. I'm really sorry to disappoint you. I wanted to see that supermoon!"

I look at Leo and Tinsley, who also seem disappointed. I get a little panicky rush, afraid this will be the end of the line. And I feel a little silly for thinking it, but the fear is there: What if this was the only reason they were being friends with me? Everything we've been doing together was so I could find the castle; we've *got* to go looking for a castle. Plan B starts forming in my mind.

"It's fine, Dad. I understand," I say.

"Oh good. I hated to let you down when I know how much you miss Mom and hiking with her. But this just gives us more time to plan," Dad says. "It'll be a great trip." He gives me a quick, dusty hug. "Why don't you three help yourself to some lunch?"

"Actually, I have to head home," Tinsley says before I even have a chance to talk about the hike. "Promised Dad we'd do some sudoku today. But I'll be back!"

We say goodbye, and Leo and I head to the bus to make grilled cheese sandwiches. I don't say anything about the hike being canceled because I'm still thinking about how to make it happen. Leo doesn't seem disappointed, and after we eat he still wants to hang out and look through the photos of the kings' book on my phone, and compare symbols to see if we can find any connection. There are some similarities, but no way to figure out what they mean since everything is in Latin. Suddenly, a shiny black car with tinted windows pulls into the driveway. I slide the map into the book about Annie that Mom bought me, and we peek out the windows as a man in a suit gets out of the back seat.

"That's Mr. Sanders," Leo says, looking at me like I have any idea why Mr. Sanders would be here. I shrug, but slide the window open all the way so we can listen to him and Dad.

Mr. Sanders holds out his hand. "Kip Moser, nice to meet you. David."

My dad politely shakes David Sanders's hand, but I can tell by his expression that he's a little suspicious. "What can I do for you?"

"I've been hearing a lot about the progress here and wanted to come see for myself. My firm may be interested in purchasing once you're finished." Mr. Sanders looks up at the purple house. "She's a beauty, isn't she? Lots of history here."

Dad nods and crosses his arms over his chest. "Yes. Quite a bit more work to go before there's much to see, I'm afraid."

"I'd like to have a tour, nonetheless."

My dad doesn't say anything at first. I think he's trying to figure out if Mr. Sanders is serious or not. "Oh. You mean right now?" Dad takes off his safety goggles and leads Mr. Sanders into the house.

"I told you he owns everything in town," Leo says, coming away from the window.

"It wouldn't be a bad thing if he bought it. My dad will need someone to do that when he's done. It's how his job works," I say.

"You don't know him, Lin. He treats everyone terribly. He never even said or did anything about Tinsley's dad's accident, and I heard his company won't pay for any of their medical bills even though it happened on the job." Leo shakes his head and sits back at the table. "He's bad news."

"How do you know that? About Tinsley's dad, I mean?"

"My mom—she had him as a patient when it first happened. She came home fuming."

"That's awful," I say. That must be why Tinsley and her mom do so much for him; they can't afford a nurse at home. My dad has always seemed so strong, and both my parents are really active. I can't even imagine one of them being bedridden. Or what would happen to my life if we couldn't pay medical bills. We couldn't be on the road, that's for sure. I never even thought about stuff like that.

After a long time, Dad and Mr. Sanders finally come out of the purple house. They are too far away for us to hear now, but they shake hands and then Mr. Sanders gets back in his car and leaves. We go out to ask my dad what's up.

"He's interested in purchasing this place," my dad says. He looks a little confused.

"Are you going to sell it to him?" I ask.

"He's interested in purchasing it now."

There's a strange flutter in my stomach. "But you're not even done yet," I say, my voice cracking on *done*.

"That's what I told him." Dad shakes his head. "Don't worry, I'm not selling yet. I like to see things through to the end, though he did offer quite a price." He sighs. "I don't know, something to think about." He heads back over to the door he was working on.

"You *just* got here," Leo whispers—exactly what I'm thinking.

"He said he wasn't selling," I snap back. Leo recoils, and I lower my voice. "Sorry, I didn't mean it like that. I . . . my dad *said* he wasn't going to." But my insides feel boiling hot even thinking about what happens if Dad changes his mind. I don't *want* to move again right away. And I can't believe I'm thinking that.

"If we're going to hang out the rest of the day, I'm going to have to go get the dogs," Leo says.

"Okay, I'll go with you," I say, but my mind is elsewhere as we walk. All I can think about is how my parents can make all these decisions whenever they want. They always have, and I've always been part of whatever they're doing. But what's going to stop Dad from selling the house right now and hitting the road again even if I don't want to? Dad does his thing, and now Mom does hers, and I'm supposed to go along for the ride forever? I'm like a yo-yo. It's completely unfair. I'm still carrying the Annie Smith Peck book, so I open it up to look at the map and blurt out my plan B to Leo.

"What if we go camping and search for the castle ourselves?" I ask.

"Alone?"

"Well, I'll ask Tinsley too. The three of us." I hold up the map.

"We have at least some of the directions right here." I know I could do a camping trip by myself; I don't need my dad. "All you need is a backpack and a sleeping bag. Do you have those?"

"Yeah," Leo says, but doesn't look totally thrilled. We reach his house, and he runs in to get Merlin and Little John, who come out tails wagging and wiggling all around my legs. I can't help but smile.

"Hi, furballs," I say as I scratch them.

We start to head back to my place, and I continue to try to convince Leo that going camping would be so much fun, but we're only a matter of steps away from Leo's house when suddenly someone jumps out from behind a big pickup truck parked on the side of the road. Aaron Sanders. Michael and Seth are sitting on the tailgate swinging their legs. None of them are old enough to drive, so I have no clue whose truck they're on.

"You've got to be kidding me," Leo says under his breath. He hooks the leashes onto the dogs and holds them close by his side. "My house is right there, you guys. I can see my front door. What do you want?"

Michael and Seth jump off the truck and come to Aaron's side. Three against two.

"Just droppin' in to say hi," Aaron says, grinning. He holds up his hands like a fake surrender. "You're all going camping this weekend? How cute."

Neither of us say anything. The last thing we need is the Sanders brothers in the woods anywhere near us, and it would stink if *they* were the ones to find the castle, after everything they've done to Leo. I close the book and try to hold it at my side. But it doesn't go unnoticed.

Michael slaps the book out of my hands. It hits the ground, but not before the map flutters out. "Whatcha hiding?"

"Nothing," I say. "Shopping list." I try to get to it first, but Aaron bends down and picks it up.

"Guess you didn't find anything on it since you have no bags with you." Aaron circles me. "It looks like a five-year-old drew this," he says. "What is it?"

"None of your business," I say. "It's mine." I try to snatch it back, but he's quicker.

Seth and Michael look over Aaron's shoulder. "That's the hiking trail," Seth says, glancing at me. My insides knot up. He almost seems sorry to say it out loud. A car passes by, and I think about waving them down for help, but mostly I'm frozen on the spot.

"What are you two planning up there?" Michael asks. "A romantic getaway?"

"Shut up!" Leo shouts. And then looks around like he's sorry he was so loud. But no one opens a door, no one pops out a window. It's like we're all invisible. Or maybe everyone is just not home. Either way, we are on our own.

The other boys look at him incredulously. Michael simply shoves him to the sidewalk, and he almost loses his glasses. The dogs start barking and I try to help Leo, but Michael blocks me. "Hey!" I shout. "Knock it off!" I try to help Leo, but Michael blocks me. This is exhausting. No wonder Leo has been hiding out from them for so long. Just before it seems Aaron is going to pounce on Leo, a voice booms behind all of us.

"I won't stand for bullies in Newbridge!"

We all turn and see someone dressed in a superhero costume coming toward us. With a dented metal trash can lid in one hand and swinging something in the other. And bright pink hair.

"What the . . . ?" Aaron says, and then starts laughing when he realizes it's Tinsley. "Oh my god. It's Simon's sister. Mini-Cooper!"

When she's closer I realize she's whipping a Slinky around. "I know how to use this, Aaron Sanders. Ever get a six-foot metal Slinky wrapped around your body? Well, I have, and let me tell you—" She flicks it toward the boys, who jump back. Most likely because the whole thing is so unexpected none of us know how to react.

"I'M NOT KIDDING AROUND," she shouts. "I know how to use this thing. Get out of here." She pretends to whip it in their direction again just as a car turns down our street. Finally, the three of them dip around a corner and disappear. I'm starting to get the feeling they mostly just want to torment us, not actually do anything. Regardless, now they have the map. I bend down and pick up my book, which is fortunately not damaged, and think, *This is the second time Tinsley Cooper has saved my life.*

Then I lift up our hero's eye mask. "Who are you supposed to be?"

"Geez, Lin! Captain America! Don't worry," she says. "I wouldn't have actually hit them. But I knew the Blackbeard approach would work."

"The what?"

"Blackbeard," she says. "The pirate? He mostly had a reputation because he acted insane, not because he actually did any of the things people assumed he did. Those boys are easy to scare; they're all talk."

Leo dusts himself off. "Not *all* talk."

"Are you okay?" I ask him.

"Yeah, I'm fine. But I am seriously so done with them." He leads the dogs down the sidewalk toward my place. I can tell he's really embarrassed, but at least this time he doesn't shout at me or go home. I think he knows he can trust us. I hang back with Tinsley and tell her about the map, and now how we've lost it.

"They don't even know what it's for, do they?" she asks.

"I don't think so."

"Then we're fine."

Dad is still sanding when we get back, and he waves to me and Leo but salutes Tinsley as we sit in the grass outside the bus in a circle. I bring out some veggie chips and lemonade for everyone.

"So what's the plan?" Tinsley asks. "Leo said that now you want us to go up the mountain anyway?"

"Yes." I pick white clovers out of the grass and start tying them together as we talk. "I think we should all go up on Saturday. I'm worried about them having the map. We definitely can't wait for my dad now."

"As long as Aaron and Michael don't figure out what it's for, we're okay," Leo says. "Right?"

"I'm not convinced they won't figure it out. And you're the one always talking about their dad owning everything. You know exactly what would happen if they all found the castle—Mr. Sanders would figure out a way to buy it."

Tinsley says, "Someone *has* to stand up to them and stop them."

"That would take military action," Leo says. "No one from this town is going to stand up to the Sanderses. Their dad owns, like, a dealership, three restaurants, the old mill. He wants to buy Lin's dad's house, as of today. He probably owns the post office and the police force."

"I don't think that's possible," I say. "And my dad's not going to sell yet." *I hope.* I keep tying the clovers together, and think about everything they are saying and the plan that's coming together in my head for sneaking away this weekend.

Tinsley leans over and looks at my creation. "Lin, what are you making?"

"A clover crown." I hold up the flower chain. "For Leo." I tie it together and put it on his head. He turns pink.

"Yeah, *this* would definitely keep the Sanderses away from me," he says. But he leaves it on his head.

"Can you make me one too?" Tinsley asks.

"Yep," I say, and start on a second. "The only thing we can do is get to the castle first. I'll film the entire thing so I'll get to make my movie and prove that we got there first."

Leo lies back in the grass and folds his hands over his chest. "But we don't know if it's definitely real or anything."

"The only way to find out is to try," I say as I tie Tinsley's crown together, stand up, and place it on her head. It's an interesting accessory to her superhero costume.

She gently touches it and says, "Now make one for yourself so we all match."

I gather more flowers. "You both have to come. We will all just need a good cover-up plan, because my dad was pretty sure it would be an overnight trip." When I look up from the ground, both Leo and Tinsley look surprised. "What?" I ask.

"It's just, well, I wasn't sure that you wanted company," Leo says.

"Same," says Tinsley. "You seemed like you were going on a solo trip to make your movie."

I realize I never even officially invited Tinsley to go with us, and although Dad mentioned hiking to everyone, we hadn't actually made plans to find the castle all together. I've just been on a mission to figure everything out, and Leo and Tinsley have been along for the ride. "Of course I want you to go with me! You do want to, right?"

"Yes!" Tinsley shouts. "You too, Leo, right?"

Leo looks at us both for a second and seems like he's afraid to say his own answer. "I really do too."

"Okay, good! You could both tell your parents we're having a campout here," I say. "And I'll tell my dad I'm at your house for a pool party and sleepover, Tinsley. And that I'm going over early to help you set up, because we're going to have to leave first thing in the morning." As I tie the clovers, my hands tremble a little bit. This would be a very big lie, not like sneaking out the other night, which was big enough.

I put the last crown on my head. "It won't be the same if you can't go with us," I say to Leo. "You have to ask your mom if you can stay over at my place."

He looks at me like he's grateful, like maybe no one has ever wanted him to go somewhere with them. He takes a deep breath. "I'll figure it out," he says. "I'm in." He puts one hand out. Tinsley puts hers on top of his. And I put mine on top of both.

"'It's a dangerous business going out your front door,'" Leo says with a really bad British accent. "Or something like that. That's from *Lord of the Rings*," he adds. We all laugh.

"Nice. I don't know about dangerous," I say. "But this will definitely be an epic adventure. For all of us. Leo, because you love King Arthur. Tinsley, because your dad always hoped to go look for it, and for me because . . ." I pause, because I'm so excited it feels like my heart is beating too fast, and I'm trying to find the right words to say "I need an adventure" without sounding too much like a dork.

Leo finishes my sentence for me. "Because it would mean you're just like your mom?"

I look at him for a minute, trying to decide if he's right or not. Part of me thinks he might be. It's a strange feeling to admire someone for doing something you're also upset about. Mom had to leave me behind to do work she loves, the work that makes me so proud she's my mom, and yet there's still part of me that feels utterly forgotten. Unimportant.

"Because it's important," I say. "Finding the castle could answer a century of questions."

Leo and Tinsley both grin. "I like the sound of that," Tinsley says.

"Only two more sleeps until we embark," I say. "The mountains are calling." Actually, that's some famous explorer's quote, but I don't mention it.

I just claim it for myself.

PART TWO

10

Less than forty-eight hours later, we're standing at the entrance to the Appalachian Trail near the majestic Delaware Water Gap. The AT only crosses through a very small part of New Jersey, only ten of the over two thousand total miles that go from Maine to Georgia, and the New Jersey section happens to start right next to Newbridge.

I pan my camera over the entrance to a whole new world. I don't want to admit it to my parents, but I guess they were right: You can explore anywhere. Now it's up to me to prove it to Mom that I really am her "future mountaineer."

"Hey, Lin?" Leo waves his hand in front of the camera. "Are we hiking or not?"

"Oh, sorry." I click off the camera. "I was just getting some footage of the trail and brainstorming my opening voice-over for the movie." It's dawn, and the bit of dappled early yellow light through the trees makes me feel like it's a morning of possibilities. We are each equipped with a backpack of supplies, and a light sleeping bag—which I showed

Leo and Tinsley how to roll tightly so that they could attach it to their backpacks. Since we've only planned to be gone one night, we brought the bare essentials—water, oatmeal, beef jerky (for Leo and Tinsley), protein bars, a few clementines, the rest of the fried plantains, almond butter and bread, and marshmallows, because Tinsley insisted camping wasn't camping without a campfire and toasted marshmallows.

"Tinsley, you have a flashlight?" I ask.

Tinsley nods. This is the first time I've ever seen her in regular clothes, although they are the most mismatched clothes I can imagine, right down to her socks, one of which is green and the other red. "Yes, Captain Moser."

"I'm not a captain," I say.

"What do you call the person in charge of a climbing team?"

"I guess just the leader."

I turn to Leo. "Are you ready?" Working up to this morning, he had been extremely nervous about the whole thing. I think we all have been. Even I was walking around the bus as if the floor was thin ice, afraid my face would give away the whole thing to my dad. But as late as last night I thought for sure Leo was going to back out. He texted me pretty much every "what if" question you could possibly come up with for a hike.

What if we see a bear?

What if it thunderstorms?

What if we get lost?

Of course, I had an answer for every single thing. Who does he think I am?

Me:

Bear: Make a lot of noise. They are afraid of people.

Thunderstorm: Crouch under bushes. Never by trees.

Lost: I have a compass, and I know how to use it. We won't get lost.

Him:

Hard to argue with you.

Me:

You're going to be great. And trust me, you're going to love it.

The last text he sent was a mountain emoji and a thumbs-up. Now, standing here, he fiddles with the zipper on his bag for a minute, but then he looks directly at me and says, "I'm ready."

"This is your last chance to change your mind," I say. "I don't want either of you to feel pressured, because we will probably all be in big trouble tomorrow when we get home."

Tinsley shrugs. "I'm never pressured."

Leo looks at her like he can't decide if she's lying or amazing. Probably a little bit of both. "I'm good," he says. "I'm tired of always being afraid to go out my front door, and I'm tired of my mom not letting me go out the front door. I will deal with whatever happens."

"Okay," I say. "Then into the woods we go!" I step onto the trail, leading our group up the steep, lush hillside.

Tinsley starts singing a song about going into the woods, and Leo sighs. "This is going to be a long walk," he jokes.

"Come on," Tinsley says. "I'll teach you the words."

I'm so excited it's hard to not run. But I know we probably have a long way to go. It's five miles just to the first landmark Mr. Holiday gave us, the rhododendron grove. I think that alone will take us about two hours, so we have to take our time. Save energy. Slow and steady. I plan on recording as much as I can of our hike, but I don't want the camera to die, so I'm going to space it out a bit and wait for each milestone, like the grove and the boulders. That should give me a nice montage of important moments leading up to the big finale: finding the castle. It's just like how Mom does many of her videos.

Before Virginia, we were in Utah, and between filming for *Moseying*, Mom and I would take trips out to Bryce Canyon so she could get video of the red rocks that are stacked like messy Jenga towers. She said all films, whether they are two hours or five minutes, have to tell a story. They have to build to one important turning point, and sometimes a montage is the best way to do that in a short time. As we walk, I plan and edit it in my head, imagining the climactic moment of discovering the castle. She will be so proud.

None of us say much for a long time, other than Tinsley's song and her attempting to teach Leo the lyrics. We mostly focus on walking. Crunching leaves and twigs, an occasional sparrow song, and cars on the distant highway are the only sounds. I keep thinking about Mom on her own adventure right now. Over the past couple of nights, I finished the Annie Smith Peck book—it kept me from getting too nervous about leaving for the hike—and she went on so many of her own as well. According to that book, she made her first expedition sometime in her thirties. She climbed huge summits in Europe and Peru as well as all over the United States. But when she was my age, I'm sure she roamed the woods and trails near her home, and if she'd lived here, she'd have definitely looked for the castle. I bet she explored everything on her own even when people thought she shouldn't. Maybe sometimes she even took friends with her on expeditions, friends who didn't think she was weird because she knew so much about the outdoors and not so much about parties or how to apply nail polish. Although I do want to go to parties and learn how to apply nail polish. Why not have both adventures in the natural world and fun at home?

"Tinsley?"

"Uh-huh?"

"Do you think when we get back from this, I mean after we're done being grounded for, like, the rest of our lives, you could teach me how to put on nail polish?"

"You don't know how to paint your nails?" she asks without sounding like she's judging me for it.

"I've never tried. I mean, I could probably figure it out on my own—"

"No, I'll definitely show you! I could dye your hair if you

want too! You'd look amazing with purple streaks through your braids." She catches up to me and explains how she dyed her own hair leaning over the bathroom sink and made an enormous mess.

"The sink was pink for weeks," she says. "My mom was so mad. It's much better to have help. We could even do it in your yard; it doesn't have to be inside." She turns to Leo. "We could do yours too! Oh, Leo, you'd look good with red! We could have a big dye party!"

"Uh, that's okay," he says. "Not sure colorful hair is my thing."

"How about your nails? I could paint them black or, better yet, blue," Tinsley says. "Blue would look awesome."

"Why do you want to color everything?"

"Because it's fun. And it doesn't last forever. You can try different things, you know."

"I guess you can paint my nails. But not my hair."

Tinsley punches the air. "Yes! I've converted you both now!"

I laugh. "Converted us to what?"

"People who have fun."

"I have fun!" Leo and I both shout at the same time.

"Okay," Tinsley reconsiders. "People who *look* fun." She grins.

Leo smacks at the tree trunks with a stick. "You know, you don't have to dress so wild or paint everything to look fun. I mean, it *is* fun, but you're just fun anyway."

"That's the nicest thing you've ever said, Leo Martin!" Tinsley grabs Leo's hand and squeezes it before she lets go and keeps skipping forward. He looks like he might die right there on the trail. "I like to take it far, though. I want to be noticed."

"No one could possibly not notice you, Tinsley," I say.

She shrugs. "Lately it doesn't feel like it. Everyone's pretty preoccupied with my dad and all, you know?"

Leo, hardly recovered from Tinsley's friendly squeeze, looks at the ground as he walks but says nothing. I'm not sure what to say, so I say, "I bet that's hard."

"I don't mean to be selfish, but yeah, it is. And Simon has always been the golden child. I guess it's not that they don't notice me, they just don't *get* me. I could give you a lot of examples, but I'd rather talk about what color we're going to paint your nails."

"If it makes you feel any better," Leo says, "we get you, right, Lin?"

"Totally. We don't have to all be exactly the same. I bet your parents wish they were like you."

"Thanks, you guys." Tinsley grins. "But I don't want to be so serious, okay? This is supposed to be fun! So, nails. Purple, I think."

We continue on for a long time, talking about nails and hair and then move on to other fun stuff that Leo also likes, like books we've read and movies I haven't seen. Tinsley can't get over the fact that I haven't seen any of the Avengers movies.

"I saw the Star Wars movie," I say in my defense.

"Which one?" Leo asks.

"There's more than one?"

He smacks his forehead. "You really have been living in a bubble!"

"We don't watch much TV as a family, and when we do it's almost always documentaries or old shows my parents like." It occurs to me for the first time that other families might do things completely different. Once my parents took me to a drive-in movie. I think I was around seven and we were living in Illinois. Those were the early days, before *Moseying* really took off. We saw some Disney movie that I don't even remember what it was about because I was obsessed over the fact that the animals weren't the right colors and they were talking. I wouldn't stop asking questions. Dad got so frustrated we ended up leaving before it was over and got ice cream instead. "This is *your* fault," he teased Mom.

Come to think of it, ice cream must be Dad's favorite trick.

"Maybe we can have some movie parties too, and you both can catch me up?" I ask.

Leo looks super excited about this idea, and launches into an enormous list of which movies I have to see and in what order. "You're definitely watching all the Marvel movies and in the proper order."

"What's the proper order?" Tinsley asks. "Shouldn't she just watch them in the order they came out?"

Leo drops his head back and sighs. "You don't know the true

order?" He then launches into a long—honestly impressive—presentation about the Marvel universe and the proper order of all twenty-three (so far) movies, which is apparently not related to when they actually came out in theaters but when the superhero character existed in time.

When he's done, Tinsley says, "Okay, nerd. You win."

I have no idea what he's talking about, but all I can think is Leo is exactly like me. Different obsessions, same devotion.

"Hey, you guys want to take a break and have a snack?" I ask. We've been walking for two hours already, which is great news because we have to be getting close to the rhododendron grove, but my stomach is growling. I find a nice fallen tree for us to sit on and pull the jar of almond butter out of my bag. Tinsley has the bread and a plastic knife. We make ourselves little sandwiches, and with the cold water in my canteen, nothing has ever tasted better. A sparrow flits around us from branch to branch as though it's waiting for us to drop crumbs.

"Hiking makes me hungry," Tinsley says.

"And tired," Leo says.

"Leo," I ask between bites, still thinking about how similar we are, "what happened with those Sanders boys? Why are they always bothering you?"

Leo chews for a minute and seems like he's about to finally tell me when suddenly two men appear out of nowhere on the trail. We all freeze.

"Hi there!" One of the guys waves. They both look around,

and the other says, "Hey, everything okay here? Are you kids lost?"

We're *just* getting started. And so far this is the best day since the day my family got here. The last thing we need is for grown-ups to report us and ruin everything.

11

I've told more lies this week than in my entire life, and it's starting to weigh on me by this point. But in my defense, there is no other way around it. Desperate times call for desperate measures! If I tell these hikers the truth, that we're alone, they're likely to be worried and want to call our parents or walk us back to town.

So I continue my streak.

"My dad is right off the trail a bit," I say, holding my hand up to my mouth like it's a private conversation. "Using the little boys' room."

The men nod. "Gotcha. When nature calls . . ." They wish us happy trails and continue on their way.

Once they're out of earshot, Leo says, "That was quick thinking."

"It just came to me." I start packing up the lunch supplies and try to push it out of my head that there's a chance I've made a bad decision. Regardless, we're going to keep going. Mom says it's not so much about making a right decision as living with the consequence. *Can you live with it?* I hear her in my head, and decide that yes, I can.

"Let's move before we run into too many other hikers," I tell my friends. "The trail is going to get busier as the day goes on, and I want to get off it before that happens."

Leo and Tinsley finish their sandwiches, and then in no time we're walking again. I know the grove has to be close because, according to my phone, we've walked over four miles. Part of me worries, though, that Mr. Holiday didn't remember correctly, that maybe it was a lot more than five miles. There's really no way for us to know except to keep walking.

"So," Tinsley asks, "what *do* you do if you have to go to the bathroom while you're camping in the woods? Asking for a friend."

"Dig a hole," I say.

"Oh god," Leo says.

"It's not a big deal. Thru-hikers always do it. I brought toilet—"

"OKAY, STOP!" Leo covers his ears.

Tinsley tries to force his hands away. "It's just *nature*, Leonardo!" They play-wrestle for a couple of minutes, with Tinsley shouting bathroom vocabulary words every two seconds. "Just pretend you're one of the bears pooping in the woods!"

"I will not!" Leo says, still trying to escape Tinsley. "Stop being so gross."

I'm laughing so much it's hard to walk. But then right up ahead, I see it.

The grove.

I instantly turn on the camera as I approach it. It's stunning. The rhododendrons are in full bloom; giant clusters of lavender blossoms cover the broad evergreen bushes like purple clouds. White pines have left a carpet of orange needles on the path. Bumblebees hover over the flowers, barely stirring as I walk into their realm; only their soft buzzing sounds all around me. I get a close-up of the gentle bumbles, and they aren't bothered in the least by my camera. And the tall bushes seemingly go on forever, lining each side of the trail like a magical entrance to the rest of the forest. But this is our stepping-off point.

From here, we make our own way.

With my camera on all of us now, I pull my compass out of my pocket and find north. "Okay, you two. We're here."

They finally stop wrestling and look up. "Ohhhh," Tinsley says. "How beautiful. Where did those flowers come from?"

"The ground?" Leo teases. Tinsley punches his arm.

"They just grow here, I guess," I say. Suddenly I hear what sounds like footsteps on the trail, and something jingling. Sounds like keys. "Shhhh!" I put my finger to my lips, and they freeze. Probably more hikers approaching, just as I feared. I let the camera hang around my neck and wave Leo and Tinsley over, and we quickly duck into the bushes and push our way through the twisted, gnarly branches. Whoever was on the trail sounds like they're right behind us. I gently push Leo forward and whisper, "Go, hurry! I don't want anyone to see what direction we go."

Branches smack our faces and crack and shake behind us the entire way until we trip out the other side, all of us tangled together from moving so fast, and we fall on our butts in a pile. I pull myself out from underneath them and whip around. I don't know who I was expecting to be standing there, but it wasn't two furry dogs.

Merlin and Little John.

Leo jumps up immediately. "Good boys." He pulls them close to us, and we all give them good scratches. They have collars on, which is what I heard jingle, but of course no leashes. "How did you two get up here?" Leo asks as we all pet them.

"On the trail," Tinsley says and sticks her tongue out at him.

"Ha ha." He looks at me. "This is not good. I don't know how they got out of the yard."

"I can't believe they followed us all the way here," Tinsley says. "That's amazing."

"What do you want to do?" I ask him. *Please don't say go home.*

He scratches the dogs and presses his face into their fur. "I guess they wanted to join the quest." He smiles. "So they can go with us."

"Are you sure?" I ask. "They won't run off?"

Leo shakes his head. "No, you know them. They're smart. They don't like being away from me and Mom, which is probably why they escaped to follow."

"Can they also open gates?" Tinsley asks.

"No, I guess I didn't shut it all the way when I sneaked out," Leo says.

"We have plenty of food and water to share, and we'll be home tomorrow anyway," I say. It will be nice to have their company while we camp out also. I get a quick scan of the forest ahead of us. Without a trail, it feels a little less friendly, but it's not too thick with trees and underbrush that we can't make our way through. *Five miles to the rhododendrons and then head north to the rock scramble.* Mr. Holiday's words are burned in my memory by now. Hopefully they continue to be correct. I reach into my backpack for the scraps of fabric I tore from a bright red T-shirt last night.

"What are those for?" Leo asks.

"To mark the trail from here on out," I say as I tie one scrap on a rhododendron branch. "This way we'll have a better idea of how to get home."

"Smart!" Tinsley says. "Like Hansel and Gretel."

"Minus the birds eating the crumbs and the old lady cooking us for dinner," Leo says.

"Exactly. Ready?" I ask my team, and point. "We're heading north."

Merlin and Little John jump over logs and leap from rock

to rock; we humans are more careful about not twisting an ankle between the stones. The dogs seem like they were made for the woods despite living in town. The forest floor is extremely rocky, though, so I pick up a thick branch and break off smaller twigs until I have a nice walking stick. Leo and Tinsley do the same, and it makes it a little easier getting over the uneven ground.

We're quietly moving on when out of nowhere Leo says, "Do you want me to answer your question from before, Lin?" He sounds unsure, but I do. I really do.

"Yes, if you want to tell me."

He pauses for a minute. "I do. I just don't talk about it much. But last year, Aaron and Michael Sanders, and some of their friends, had a game in the cafeteria where they'd put their hands on the seats before the girls sat down, so they could, you know . . ."

I stop in my tracks and turn around. It takes me only a second to understand what he's saying, but it makes me realize there's a lot more to school that I've not known about. "Wait. What?"

Tinsley looks at me. "It was really awful. They would *not* stop. Most of the girls would move in huge groups, hoping to keep them away."

"Lots of kids told on them, but when I told on them, they were suspended for a long time, which, if you know the Sanderses, just doesn't happen."

"And they came after you?"

Leo sighs. "They caught me after school one day, and let's just say I'm no ultimate fighter. And ever since, if I'm in the same room as them, they are on me immediately, so I ate lunch with Mrs. Bower, my English teacher, and never walked the halls alone. And my mom . . . well, she's always been protective and nervous, but after that, she wouldn't let me leave the house alone for a long time."

For once I'm the speechless one. I look at Tinsley, and she makes a face like, *Yeah, it's all true*.

Leo pushes up his glasses, looks at the ground, and starts walking again. "You asked. You wanted to know what happened. That's what happened."

"I . . . I did, I just . . . I wasn't expecting *that*." I follow him. "That's awful. What they were doing to girls and to you. I'm sorry. I had no idea."

"You weren't here. Why would you know?"

I don't have an answer because he's right, I've clearly lived in some bubble my entire life. And the past few weeks, complaining about my own problems, which don't seem anywhere near as big now.

"Leo, I'm sorry I didn't say anything to you either," Tinsley says. "I knew. It was too weird to talk about because Simon got in trouble too. You did the right thing by telling on them."

"It doesn't feel like it," Leo mumbles.

"Simon was part of it?" I ask.

"He insists he was not," Tinsley says. "That's why he's no longer friends with the Sanderses."

"Yeah, so they brought Seth into their fold instead," Leo says bitterly.

"Why didn't the teachers stop them?" I ask.

"They're too smart to get caught," Leo says. "Besides, teachers are afraid of their dad. And I'm not saying anything about them ever again. I just have to survive until they give up and move on to someone else."

I don't say it out loud, but I don't think that's a good plan. Leo's life shouldn't be miserable because of them. We keep walking for a long time without speaking. Every now and then I tie a red scrap to a branch. I try to space them out as far as possible to make them last but make sure I can still see the last one I've tied before I tie the next. Tinsley and I fall back from Leo just a little bit. She holds on to my forearm as she talks. "I figured it was better he told you himself," she whispers. "I hope that's okay."

"Yeah, I totally get it."

"Honestly, I wasn't sure if he was going to blame Simon for being part of it too."

"You think Simon is telling the truth?"

Tinsley nods. "I'm positive."

"That's good."

"Are you okay?" she asks me.

I think about that question for a second. I miss my mom. Mom would know what to do or say right now to help Leo get out of this situation, and I definitively do not. "Sorry. I was just thinking about my mom. Random, I know. Usually we hike together, so I was thinking about that."

"It's okay," Tinsley says. "I'd love to do stuff like that with my mom."

"Maybe when your dad's better?" I ask.

"She's not really into music or theater. Before Dad's accident, she sold insurance."

"Oh."

Tinsley points up ahead to where Leo is standing at the base of the rock scramble in a victory pose. "Look! There it is!" she says, and jogs to catch up to him. She has a talent for changing the subject. I want to tell her that it's kind of like that with my dad too, that we don't love the same things either, but we find other ways to have fun together, like playing games or building a campfire. But she's absorbed in the massive pile of boulders before us that we have to scale.

I get a quick video before we start. It's a hillside of huge stones, almost like someone plowed them all up and over the ridge. And we have to scramble over them to get up. I've been on harder climbs with Mom, but this will be a first for Leo and Tinsley, and suddenly I realize *I'm* the responsible one. Not Mom.

"This is going to be challenging," I say. "But we can do it. Can the dogs do it?"

Little John jumps up onto a boulder and Merlin follows.

Leo laughs. "I think they're part mountain goat."

The dogs seem to already know exactly where we are going and practice jumping across rocks. They look back at us and bark.

"I guess that's our cue to follow!" I say, and we begin our climb.

12

What started out as a fun challenge becomes tiring very quickly. We have to use our whole bodies to haul ourselves over each rock, so I can't film any of our ascent, but it is quite a feat. Mr. Holiday wasn't kidding when he said we needed adult strength. But we manage it, even if it's slow. Some of the boulders are easier to leap to, but there are some huge ones that require us to find hand- and footholds and pull ourselves up and over like we're rock climbing. At one point I look back and realize we're only about halfway up even though my body is telling me I need to be done.

I sit on a big flat rock to catch my breath. Leo and Tinsley do the same. Only the dogs seem unbothered. They are way better at this than us in finding ways around the biggest boulders, and actually reach the top while we take a water break.

Leo shouts up to them, "Stay there! We're coming!"

"Lucky dogs with four legs," Tinsley says. "Show-offs."

"How are you guys feeling?" I ask.

"I'm good," Leo says after a big gulp of water.

"Tinsley?"

"My thighs and calves hate you right now, but I'm otherwise good."

"Well, mine hate me too, so that's fair." I put my canteen away and stand up. "Let's finish this."

It takes us about twenty minutes to finally reach the top. I get the camera going, now that my hands are free, and I film the view in all directions. It would be amazing if we could just see the castle from this spot, but ahead of us lies never-ending rolling hills and valleys and a lot of continued rocky ground. The sun is high in the sky now, and hot on the top of the ridge where there are fewer trees to shade us. Out of breath, sweaty, and thirsty, we turn around to survey our accomplishment. We are really high up. It occurs to me it will be much harder going back down, but we'll worry about that tomorrow.

Right now, we are victors and it feels amazing! It's like when Mom and I kayaked for the first time. She said she was so out of her element; she was a mountain girl. But together we did it.

I aim the camera at Leo and Tinsley. "We made it through together! So, anything to say about the expedition so far?"

"I think I'm actually really enjoying this," Leo says, breathing hard. "But that castle better be waiting for us."

Tinsley nods. "It is waiting for us, Leo. And we will find it. We could never have done this without you, Lin."

I lower the camera. Something in her voice makes me realize this is way more important to her than I knew, but also makes me think, *If we don't find it, will she still be so grateful?* "Yes, you could," I say. "But thank you."

"I mean, you had all the camping equipment, after all," Tinsley teases. We all laugh, and I turn off the camera to consider our next step.

"Now we keep heading north and look for the boulder tower. Mr. Holiday has had an amazing memory so far, so I'm sure this next bit will be a cinch," I say, taking a quick look at the picture of the map on my phone.

"Wait, who is *that*?" Tinsley asks, and points at the base of the scramble. "Is that who I think it is?"

A boy stands at the bottom, who's then joined by a second and third. One of them waves like they're in a parade. Aaron, Michael, and Seth.

"No freaking way," Leo says. "They're following us?"

"Maybe they're the ones who let Merlin and Little John out," I wonder out loud. If they did, I have to give them more credit than I want to. Of course the dogs would lead them right to Leo, and Seth knew the map was for the trail. It would be an easy way to track us, and smarter than I'd thought. But why? Why go so far just to torment poor Leo? I can't imagine having nothing better in my life to do than to chase other kids in the woods.

Leo looks at me, shocked. "If they did, I'll—" He makes a fist but doesn't finish his thought.

"What are we going to do now?" Tinsley asks.

"We run that way and don't stop until we have to." I take off, and the two of them follow. Our only hope is to get as far away from the Sanderses as possible so they can't see us. It should be easy to lose them without a trail, at least I hope. The dogs bound alongside us, completely carefree. I'm a bit jealous. The last thing we need is the Sanderses following us, or worse, *chasing* after us. After what Leo told me, I'm much more afraid of them than I was before.

We dodge beneath low branches. Jump fallen trees. Crash through ferns. Avoid a scratchy little plant called cow-itch that looks harmless but gives you a nasty burning rash. All three of us trip now and then, but nothing terrible. Branches smack my face and sides, and I scratch my arm on the rough bark of an oak. Tinsley rolls her ankle. But for the most part we seem to get pretty far away without any major injuries, and honestly, the whole thing is kind of exhilarating! We don't stop until Leo signals that he's done. Then we sit behind the roots of a giant fallen tree so we can all catch our breath and I can finally tie a marker.

The dogs instantly lie down next to Leo and pant themselves to sleep. I can't say I blame them. What a rush. I get the camera out and quickly film our tired team, narrating that we just narrowly escaped the Sanderses, and now we are about to embark on the next leg of the journey. "Anything you want to add?" I ask Leo and Tinsley.

"Only I really hope we're going the right way," Leo says. I don't say that I hope we are too. As a leader of an expedition, one has to be confident.

"Lin totally knows what she's doing," Tinsley says.

"I know we're going the right general direction," I say. Tinsley's unending support makes me nervous. I only know as much as Mr. Holiday told all of us, and I'm making the best choices I can.

Leo shrugs. "Think we're far enough away?"

"I hope so." I click off the camera, and check the map and time on my phone. Almost noon. I don't have any texts from Dad, but I realize there's no more service anymore either, so who knows if he's actually sent any or not. I was really hoping we'd find the boulder stack before we had to camp for the night. If the symbols are on the stone like Mr. Holiday said, and if they match up to the tapestry, that'll give us all night to try to interpret it. Although I have no idea how we're going to do that. "Let's keep going and we'll just keep an eye out."

"Of all the monsters in the woods I was preparing myself for, the Sanderses were not one of them," Tinsley says. "It's like we're being hunted."

"Geez, Tinsley," Leo says.

I shiver. The woods have never scared me before. It's always been a peaceful, beautiful place. But I've never been in the woods without my mom, and I've never been around boys like them.

After another hour of walking, and looking over our shoulders constantly, we come into a strange clearing. There are some tiny saplings and a scattering of low bushes, but it's mostly moss- and lichen-covered stone. It's as though trees and the plants that cover the forest floor everywhere else can't grow here.

"This is so pretty," Tinsley says. "And look! Turn on your camera, Lin!" She points across the clearing. Way on the other side, there are several larger boulders that seem to line the edge, like they were placed there on purpose to mark an entry between them. Two are definitely stacked in an awkward, unnatural way, but if you were hiking through you might not think much about it, especially considering the weird rock scramble that also looks out of place and *is* natural.

"I can't even believe our luck!" I say, and start filming as we get closer. "That has to be the stone stack Mr. Holiday mentioned."

"It's definitely the same spot in that photo we saw at the lodge. 'Pen's Overlook,'" Tinsley says. "Remember?"

"Yes! Now we know Mr. Holiday was right."

We jog across the clearing to the boulders and begin searching the entire surface. The stone on top looks like it's precariously balanced and walking beneath it is a little scary.

"How did someone do this?" Leo asks.

"Maybe they didn't. Maybe it's just a really weird formation, like you see out in Arizona and Utah," I say. "They look like monuments, but have just been formed over thousands of years from—" I suddenly remember the girls in the bathroom saying I was a show-off. I look at Leo and Tinsley.

"From what?" Leo says.

"Wind and sand erosion." I clear my throat. "So maybe these are left in a weird stack from glacial movement thousands of years ago. That's partly how these mountains were formed."

"How do you know all this? You're not even from here," Tinsley asks. She runs her hand over the rock, as if searching for any kind of clue or carving.

"It's basically all I've been learning my entire life," I say. "Stuff my mom teaches me while we travel."

"I can't imagine what it's like to live like that, to have your home keep changing," Leo says. "Like, do you ever get tired of it?"

I start to answer, but Tinsley says, "Wait. Can I film your answer?"

"Sure," I say, and hand her the camera. "It's a good question, Leo. Honestly, I never thought too much about it until we moved here. Which I really did not want to do at first. My home is on the road, with both my parents, you know? I never really think about it being in a single place."

Tinsley walks closer to my face, which makes me laugh. "You can zoom like this," I say, and show her how to use the buttons.

"Ohhh!" she says, and then gets back to interviewing me. Which, I have to admit, is kind of fun. I'm not used to being on this side of the camera as much. Must be what it feels like for Dad. "So," Tinsley continues. "For most of us, home is a single place. But you think home is on the road. Can you elaborate?"

She sounds like she's trying to be a super-professional

reporter, but it cracks me up. Through laughter I say, "Not on the road, necessarily. Home is just wherever we are."

Saying it out loud is like a gut punch. That's exactly it. I didn't even realize it until I heard myself say it. Home is wherever we are, yes, but more specifically wherever *Mom* is. It's not so much New Jersey or the lack of exciting parks or adventures or whatever, it's that without Mom, it doesn't feel like *home*. I pretend to cough and hold up a finger for her to give me a second. I'm not saying any of this on camera. Once I'm convinced my face is showing nothing but confidence and excitement, I say, "So, you want to hear something else cool about these mountains I learned?"

"Lights, camera, action!" Tinsley directs. I refocus my attention on her.

"Millions of years ago when the continents were all one giant landmass, the Appalachian Mountains would have continued into the Scottish Highlands, so in some ways the trail here connects to Scotland. Just, now, you'd have to walk under the ocean for a long time."

Leo and Tinsley laugh. But not *at* me, which is a nice change from those girls in the bathroom.

"My family has a lot of Scottish heritage," Tinsley says.

"Kind of makes sense there's a castle here, then too, don't you think?" Leo says. "Just like Scotland."

"Well, the mountains would have been all one ridge millions of years ago, before people and castles," I say, "but it is kind of cool to think of how we're still connected by them." Just then, in a little crevice, I notice something. An etching that would be incredibly hard to see if you weren't looking for it.

"Guys! Look!" I point it out. "Tinsley, get the camera on this."

It's several symbols. Squares, circles, wavy lines, and a lot of arrows. It doesn't look like a language, though. It's more like little pictures you might see on the cave wall of an early civilization.

"Are these the same symbols as on the tapestry?" Leo asks. I pull out my phone and find the picture of it. Zooming in, we look closer at the center design, but they don't match. The tapestry symbols are very intricate, like they might be their own alphabet. But these are pretty simple shapes, more like road signs.

"Huh, I thought for sure they would be the same," I say, and take a few pictures of the carvings with my phone.

Tinsley hands me back the camera and quietly asks, "Now what?"

"I'm not sure. I thought this would make something clear to us." We sit for a few minutes, talking over the designs on the rock, but nothing really makes sense. "I guess we will camp here for the night. Seems like a pretty hidden spot back here behind these rocks."

Hopefully something will make sense soon. Leo and Tinsley are depending on me, and we've come all this way, risked getting in the trouble of our lives. It can't be all for nothing.

"It'll be okay," Tinsley says. "We'll figure it out."

"Mr. Holiday never did," I say as I begin gathering small twigs for kindling. "And he's lived here his whole life."

Leo makes a campfire ring with large rocks, and we clear the space of leaves and anything that might catch fire. "But at the same time, he said he only came up here twice, and it was the second time he found this rock. He didn't try all that hard to figure it out."

"True," I say as I set up the sticks in sort of a tent shape and we use leaves and some toilet paper to get the fire started. "And as far as we know, he's the only one who even got this far, right?" It doesn't take long at all before we have a small campfire.

"Maybe," Leo says. "Nothing in any of those articles even mentioned carvings on rocks."

"I'm starving," Tinsley interrupts. "What are we making?"

"Pretty much just snacking on this stuff." I toss out bags of beef jerky, granola, and the marshmallows. "There's plenty of bread for almond butter sandwiches too." The bread is a little squished, but still works. I open the photo of the tapestry and rock carvings to compare them, and nibble on a protein bar while Leo and Tinsley put together sandwiches.

"You don't want one?" Leo asks, holding up the bread.

I shake my head. "I'm good."

"I'm happy to live on toasted marshmallows alone," Tinsley says. "But I have a genius idea." She breaks a small, green branch off a nearby tree and sticks a marshmallow on the end. In about three seconds she has a flaming inferno and charcoaled lump. "Perfect." Then she squeezes it between bread smothered with almond butter.

"I changed my mind. Can you make me one of those?" I ask, and she gladly obliges.

Leo gives the dogs water and several pieces of jerky. "Do you think the smoke will give us away?"

"To the Sanderses?" I ask. "I didn't think of that."

Tinsley has sticky strings of melted marshmallow all over her hands and dripping from her chin as she tries to talk. "Are they really that smart?" she asks. "They probably went home by now. I don't think they even had bags with them. Would be stupid to keep following us."

"I agree," I say, turning the phone in various angles. No matter what direction I hold the symbols they just don't match to the tapestry. "The design on the tapestry looks like letters from a language, a language that was in the kings' book or something, but this carving is totally different. I'm not sure how it's all connected."

Leo reaches out for the phone, and I hand it to him. After a minute he says, "You know, the ones on the rock look sort of like the symbols you see in map legends. Here, look." He hands me back the phone, reaches into his bag, and pulls out *The Sword in the Stone*.

"You brought a book?" Tinsley asks. "When in the world did you think you'd have a chance to read?"

"You should always have a book with you," Leo says very seriously. "Just in case."

"Such a nerd," Tinsley says.

Leo opens to the first few pages and then hands me the book. "Check out the map legend in this." He points to the symbols. Some look very similar to the carving—triangles mean mountains, squares for buildings, etc. . . .

"So you're saying you think these are part of a map?" I ask.

"Or," Leo says, "they *are* the map. Maybe they are the directions. Look at the order. Circles, arrow, wavy lines, arrow, and so on."

"Leo, I think you might be right." I get up and snap a couple of branches off for me and Leo to toast marshmallows before Tinsley eats them all. "Mr. Holiday seemed to think it was a language, but the symbols might simply stand for something out here, like landmarks." I wave my hand. *Out here* is vast, and the landmarks could be anything. I sigh and put my marshmallow close to the embers.

The sun has gone below the mountain ridge, and a few owl calls in the distance cause the dogs to perk up. Merlin, especially, listens to everything with his back to us, and watches through the trees as if he sees something out there. Or is just prepared if he does.

I put a few more big branches on the fire to keep it going as we talk about what we think the symbols might stand for. We all unroll our sleeping bags around the campfire with our backs to the giant boulders. It feels cozy and safe, especially with the dogs keeping watch.

And then I notice the supermoon beginning to rise, taking

the place of the sun and seeming nearly as bright. It's too bad Dad's missing this. I get my camera out and film a bit of the massive orb so I can show him later. Dad loves the night sky like Mom loves the turtles. Suddenly it makes me a little sad that they both aren't on this hike with me. I thought going on my own would make me feel independent and proud, and it mostly has, but I'm also a little sad they're missing this. There's something special about sharing what you love with people who love it just as much.

Although as I aim my camera at Tinsley and Leo as they continue to look at the carvings, the moonlight reflecting off their faces, I think maybe I have found two more people who do. I put the camera away and lie down facing them.

"These are definitely arrows. They might mean to turn left or right," Tinsley suggests. She leans on her elbows, facing me, and the fire lights up her face. "I mean, it could be that simple, couldn't it?"

"Then what would the up and down arrows stand for?" Leo says.

"Hm." Tinsley puts her chin in her hand. "Good point."

It suddenly comes to me. "Compass directions," I say. "Maybe they are turns like Tinsley said, but rather than left and right, they stand for north, south, east, west."

"Riiiight," Leo says. "So all we have to do is go to the big sun and turn east, go to that blobby cloud-looking thing and turn north, go to this squiggle and turn west," he says sarcastically. He lies on his back, hands folded over his chest, on the other side of me. He's right. The symbols are so simple, it actually makes them more confusing.

"Something like that," I say. "I'm serious, though. All these other symbols—circles, triangles, blobs—must be natural landmarks, because there's nothing else up here."

"Then the circles have to be boulders," Tinsley says.

"Why?"

"Because if this is a set of directions, we can probably assume they are in order, right? And the circles are first, and that's where we're at." She points to the giant round boulders behind us.

"Good point. I was thinking the beginning was at the start of the trail, but Mr. Holiday did say that the castle is older than the trail, at least the modern trail. A lot of the original AT was formed by Native Americans. The castle was probably built somewhere in between those times, right?"

"I don't really know, but everyone always says it's at least a couple hundred years old," Leo says through a big yawn. It's not very late yet, but we got up so early and walked for so many hours. Add in the warm fire, hazy smoke, and soft moonlight softly draping over everything, and the smoky-sweet taste of toasted marshmallows, and I think all three of us are becoming drowsy. But I don't want to go to sleep until I have a good idea of what in the world we're even doing tomorrow. It's impossible to plan when you don't even know how much distance you have to cover.

We have no time to waste.

13

The next thing I know, I'm startled awake by barking dogs. The moon is far away now, so it's much darker, and other than the fire, which is just glowing embers, there's very little light. Merlin in particular is not happy.

Leo tries to shush them. I feel Tinsley move closer to me, and we both move our backs right up against the rocks. "What is it?" she asks in a muffled whisper. I'm pretty sure she has the sleeping bag over her head.

"I don't know. I didn't hear anything except the dogs," I say. I turn on my flashlight and aim it toward the trees.

"Oh god, please don't be a bear, please don't be a bear," she chants. "Please don't be a bear!"

"Bears don't come out in the middle of the night very often," I tell her. "Shhhh." I sit very still to try to see if I can hear anything other than normal night sounds like crickets, but I don't hear whatever it was the dogs heard. Pine trees creak as they gently bend with the breeze, an occasional hoot owl, some insect chirping. Spring peeper frogs. Then suddenly we hear high-pitched cries far off in the distance, which gets the dogs barking all over again.

"What *was* that?" Leo asks.

I hesitate to tell him. "Coyotes, I think."

"What?" He presses his back against the rock. "There are no coyotes in New Jersey!"

"Coyotes are everywhere. It's okay. They won't bother us. And they are super far away."

"They sound like ghosts," Tinsley says. She's got my arm in a death grip. "Like upset, shrieking ghosts."

It is sort of an eerie sound. Unnatural. A combination of a wolf howl and a hyena laugh, barking dogs and high-pitched yips. But coyotes are afraid of people. I use the words I've been raised on. "They won't bother us unless we bother them."

"I have no intention of bothering anything out here," Leo says as the barking and yappy calls rise and fall like a strangely tuned song.

"What are they doing?" Tinsley whispers. "It sounds like a whole pack."

"Probably is. I guess they're talking to one another. It sounds a little scary, but it's really not. It's like dogs playing or arguing. They're just noisy."

We listen for a while as the haunting calls echo in the dark. Merlin and Little John seem to have made peace with it as well, maybe knowing better than us what the coyotes are actually saying to one another. The faraway pack seems to quiet down after a few minutes, settling whatever business they had, probably bedding down in their cliffside dens. Soon the night is mostly silent again.

Eventually Leo and Tinsley both lie down, closer to me this time, and I wonder if this is what Mom has felt like when we camp out together. I never once considered what it's like for her watching over me, especially through the night. And we've been in far more dangerous places, as far as wildlife goes. But now I think I have an idea.

The dogs go back to sleep too, but I'm pretty sure I'm not going to fall asleep. Not because of the coyotes but because now I'm wide awake and thinking about the symbols on the rock again. I open the photo of the carving and study the symbols some more. If Tinsley's right and the circles are boulders, then triangles have to be mountains, or hills, like on a regular map. Although I guess they could also be trees, some kind of tree that would really stand out from the rest. The shape that looks like a square with an X over it has me confused. And so does one that looks a little bit like a Tetris piece. Squiggly lines is probably water, but if that means the river, it doesn't really make sense that we'd be up on the ridge and not in the valley, where the river cuts through the mountainside.

It must be a creek.

So if I'm right and the arrows are meant to be like compass directions, then we can do this. We can figure out the way to the castle. And the first stop would be a creek.

There is one last shrill howl far away, almost like a

confirmation—or maybe even a warning—that I'm on the right track.

By the time pink and orange light begins to come through the trees, I'm certain I have at least some of the symbols matched to the most likely natural landmarks that would be in these woods.

CIRCLE = BOULDER
SQUIGGLE LINES = CREEK
TRIANGLE = TREE OR A PEAK
CURVED SLOPE = STEEP HILLSIDE OR CLIFF OR CAVE
ARROWS = COMPASS DIRECTIONS

I'm not sure what the others are yet. Regardless, it's time to make a move and it's either forward or back home, so I choose forward. But my phone is close to being dead and I need to write the whole thing down on paper, or my arm, before we start off again. I didn't bring a pen, so I rummage through Tinsley's backpack to see if she brought something. She's sound asleep next to me and doesn't stir at all. It's still pretty dark, so I just have to feel around for something to write with, but I come up with nothing.

Except a folded photograph. Of a castle.

It's an old black-and-white photo, taken from a distance, almost like someone flew by and got the shot from an airplane. The castle isn't as huge as you might see in fairy tales, but it's still beautiful and intricate, with one main tower and several levels of turrets and rooms around a courtyard. The stone mansion is tucked in a rocky cliffside and looks like some of it is actually carved right from the cliff itself, like the rock swallowed the building over time. It's hard to tell how anyone could reach it other than by parachuting out of a plane. No wonder it's called "Castle in the Clouds."

But if this is *our adventure*, why does Tinsley have a picture of it and why wouldn't she have said anything? I carefully fold the photo back up, tuck it away, and close her bag. I'm not sure what to do about it, and I feel like I've been caught snooping when I shouldn't be in her bag. Tinsley is always so honest, I can't imagine she'd betray us. My heart sinks just considering that. So for now I do nothing.

Fortunately, I find a pen in Leo's bag. He wakes up as I'm transcribing the symbols across my forearm.

He yawns and sits up on an elbow. "What are you doing?"

"I thought I better write this down before my phone is totally dead. I borrowed your pen."

"Great idea. Just don't get too sweaty."

"Maybe you should put it on your arm too." I hand him the pen, and he copies the pattern to his arm. We wake up Tinsley, whose hair resembles a huge pink fluff of cotton candy.

"What?" she asks as we try not to laugh. "Oh." She touches her hair. "Lin. Leo." She throws her arms out in a glamour pose. "Meet the bedhead queen."

"That height is impressive," Leo says.

"My biggest talent." She shakes her head, bouncing her frizzy curls in all directions. "Anyone bring a hat?"

"Nope." Leo and I both shake our heads.

"Well, I guess we all have to live with a fourth member of our fellowship, my hair." Tinsley tries to pat it down, but there's no use.

We roll our sleeping bags and quickly make cold oatmeal by pouring water right in the packet before we head out. It's not the most appetizing breakfast, but it does the trick. Leo makes one for each of the dogs, and they don't seem remotely disappointed. As everyone finishes, Leo makes sure our fire is completely out and I record a little bit of our site, the boulders, Leo and Tinsley, the dogs, and all. The entire time all I can think about is the photo in Tinsley's bag. It weighs on me that I should ask her about it, but there's part of me that's a little afraid to, in case I don't like the answer.

"Starting east." I keep the camera rolling and show them on the compass which way is east. "East and west are the easiest because you can follow the sun." And aim the lens toward the rising glow behind the trees. "All right, let's do this. We have to move fast."

"How long do you think it will take to find it?" Leo asks.

"Not sure. I'm hoping only a couple of hours." Otherwise, we'll be staying overnight in the woods again, and we're not prepared for that.

But two hours later, we still haven't found the creek. And I'm beginning to think if we really want to find the castle, it's going to take more than two days. But I'm afraid to say that out loud to them because I really don't want to give up. Now that I've made it this far, I feel even more determined to find it. Dad would probably say I'm being stubborn, that determination shouldn't turn into being bullheaded, and sometimes you have to be more sensible with the way you handle something. But when did anyone sensible find a castle?

"My legs are so tired," Tinsley says as she plops down on a big rock. "Lin, I don't know how much more of this I can take."

Leo and I sit with her, and we all take a water break. We're all working with very little food and next to no sleep, so I feel her pain. But we can't give up. "I feel like we're close," I say, even though I don't feel anything except frustration and sore feet.

They both look at me like they aren't sure they believe me.

"You do think it's up here, don't you?" I ask. "I mean, both of you told *me* about it."

Leo and Tinsley look at each other and then back at me. "Well, I can't speak for Leo," Tinsley says, "but I do. I'm just really tired and afraid we won't find it in one day."

"Leo?" I ask.

He opens his mouth to answer, but a branch loudly snaps behind us before he has a chance. I swing around to see a huge buck staring right at us. I grab Leo's and Tinsley's arms. The buck's ears flick forward, a sign he's listening to us, and his tail twitches. He doesn't blink or move an inch otherwise, standing like a statue in the trees. Neither do we. He's so majestic I think all three of us hold our breath, afraid of scaring him. Very slowly, I aim the video camera at him to get a brief moment on film. His large, soft black eyes watch us intently.

The buck snorts a breathy warning at us, and then Merlin and Little John catch on and they let loose. Their urgent barking startles all of us but especially the buck, and his whole body visibly jumps.

He takes off, leaping through the woods, and vanishes in a split second, his tail a cautionary flash of white to any other deer that might be around. And then he's gone. I got it all on camera.

"Wow," Tinsley gasps. "He was huge!"

"I've never been so close to a deer like that," Leo says. "I could smell him!"

We stand and pack up our water canteens. "That was incredible," I say. "It was like he was just as interested in us as we were in him." I strap my camera across my chest, pull my bag back up on my shoulders, and decide to let Leo off the hook about whether he believes the castle is real. I'm not sure I want to know his answer anyway. "Let's keep moving."

"So we meet again!" The voice makes us all jump again. At this rate, we're going to end up having heart attacks before we reach the castle.

The Sanderses.

Leo groans and looks like he might actually pull out his hair.

Aaron grins. "You guys are exceptionally easy to track. Between a smoky campfire." He holds up a small piece of red fabric. "And this."

At first I'm not sure what I'm seeing, and then it registers that he has one of our markers in his hand: our trail home. "Please do not tell me you've taken those all down!" I say.

He reaches into his pocket and pulls out a handful of red scraps, letting them fall to the forest floor. "All these?"

I almost start crying. Or swearing. Or both. Instead, I'm shocked to silence at first and shaking with anger. He has no idea the damage he's just done. "That." I take a breath. "Was our way home. You stupid idiot."

He leaps toward me, but I waste no time and shout: "RUN!"

We scatter in three different directions. Even as I run, I know I've made the biggest mistake of our expedition so far. Weirdly, my brain goes right to my mom lecturing me about how to stay safe the very first time she and I went on an overnight together. I was around six at the time, and we were staying near Reno, Nevada. She took me up into the Sierra Nevadas, and the worst thing we ran into was poison oak. But I hear her voice in my head now, can see how serious her eyebrows are, and even though her voice is soft, she's also stern.

Other than venturing off a marked trail, separating is the worst thing you can do.

If you do get separated, stop and stay in one place. Don't panic.

Memorize your surroundings.

Only move if you're absolutely positive it's the right move.

If she were here right now, she would not be proud. But it was an instant reaction. Fight or flee, like a wild animal. And I wrongly chose to flee.

Merlin and Little John follow Leo over a small embankment. Out of the corner of my eye, I see them dive down and duck under a rocky overhang. I keep heading east, running as fast as I can, but trying not to go so far that I lose sight of where Leo hid. I even come to a creek, which I happily realize is probably the one we needed to find. Just not in these circumstances. I dive under a fallen tree that has just enough space to fit me and my bag beneath if I lie real flat. Tinsley . . . I have no idea where Tinsley goes. She seemingly vanishes into thin air. Just like the buck.

The waiting is agony. At first all I hear is my heart beating in my own ears and then the Sanderses' voices. A daddy longlegs climbs over my arm. Someone runs by but not close enough to see me. Something tickles the back of my neck, and I have to force myself not to move. Shouts seem to pop on and off around me at first, until they eventually fade completely. Still I wait a little longer, until my heart finally settles. The scent of warm, damp soil comes up from the ground as raindrops begin to split-splat on leaves. *Petrichor*, I remember my mom telling me the name for that comforting, musky scent. Big, loud, intermittent drops drown out all other sound. I put my forehead on my hands. *Mom, I wish you were here now. I don't know if I can do this alone after all.* I should have checked the weather report. Not that it would have stopped me, but we could have brought trash bags or something to stay dry.

I thought I was prepared for everything before we set out, but clearly I was wrong.

Leaves and twigs crunch near my left side, very close. Too close. Slowly I turn my head, trying not to make any sounds, expecting to see one of the brothers, or Leo or Tinsley, or even one of the dogs. But it's none of them. It's someone else entirely. I'm frozen on the spot. All I can see is a pair of brown hiking boots, camo cargo pants, and metal hiking poles walk by. It's definitely a pair of grown-up legs.

Who in the world.

I let a breath out very slowly, hoping whoever it is can't hear me. After a few more minutes, I slide out from under the tree and run back to where I saw Leo hiding. The rain falls harder now, making my braids drip down the front of my overalls. Drops hit the leaves so hard they shake and flutter in the downpour. Just as a loud rumble of thunder rolls overtop me, I drop down the embankment and duck under the rocky overhang.

Leo screams bloody murder.

"It's just me!" I put my hands up. "Sorry. I didn't mean to scare you."

He puts his hand over his chest as he catches his breath and adjusts his fogged-over glasses.

"Where's Tinsley?" we both ask at the same time.

"I thought she was with you," Leo says.

I shake my head. "I have no idea what direction she went. But I found the creek. From there we're supposed to turn north."

"Did you see where Aaron and them went?"

"No. And, Leo, there's someone else out there."

Leo's eyes open wider than they already were. "What do you mean, there's 'someone else' out there?"

"Someone else. An adult. I saw them when I was hiding."

"We have to stop," he says. "We have to go home and get help."

"Our only choice is to keep going," I say.

"Are you kidding? Tinsley is missing, and there are god knows how many people on this mountain hunting us down, and you want to *keep going*?" Leo shouts. I've never heard him be so loud before. And he looks so upset and disappointed it makes me panic a little bit. I don't really know what the best thing to do is, but we can't leave Tinsley up here *alone*, that much is true. It's Tinsley. She's all about fun and singing and dressing up. Nothing about surviving in the woods. She's completely depending on *me*. A loud crack of thunder makes both of us duck for cover. Little John whines, and Merlin moves closer.

What have I done?

The rain is deafening. For a few minutes I just listen to it. This can't be the end.

"Look," I say quietly. "If Tinsley is headed anywhere, I'm positive it's going to be toward the castle."

"How do you know?" Leo asks. "How would *she* know?"

"Because she had a photo of it in her backpack."

"What?" He gives up on his foggy glasses and takes them off to look at me. "A picture of the castle?"

"Yes. It was a really old black-and-white photo. I think it was taken from a plane."

"How do you know it's *the* castle? And why were you in her bag?"

"Pen, remember? I was just trying to find a pen, that's all." Thinking about it makes me remember the map on my arm. Now washed away from the rain. "Oh no." I grab Leo's arm to see. Half of it is smudged, half okay.

"Can you remember it?" he asks.

"I think so."

Leo gets the pen and hands it to me. I assume he's going to have me rewrite it on his arm, but instead he hands me *The Sword in the Stone*, which has managed to stay dry in his bag. "Are you sure?" I ask. "This will be permanent."

"It's okay. It will be an interesting memory."

I write down the symbols in the back on a blank page.

He closes it and slides it into his bag. "Where do you think she got it?"

"I don't have any idea. I'm more worried about the fact that she didn't tell us. And I want to know why."

"Why didn't you just ask her?"

"I was going to. I was waiting for the right time, I guess? It felt like I wasn't supposed to see it, you know?" I sit and lean against the rocks. "I thought there would be plenty of time to ask her. I didn't think she'd go missing!"

Leo sits next to me and sighs. "We have to find her."

"I know."

"And we have to figure out how to get home."

I close my eyes. "I know." I look at him, but he won't look at me.

He stares at his knees as he talks, his hands braced on his thighs almost like he's holding himself together. "Let's assume you're right, that she'd head toward the castle. She took a picture of the symbols too, right?"

"I think so," I say quietly. Something in Leo's voice is so measured, I suddenly feel like a little kid. I can tell he is *not* happy.

"Maybe her phone is still charged. We have to just hope for the best and assume she'd be looking for the creek too."

I really, really hope Leo is right. He makes me feel a little more encouraged, even though he seems upset. He's smart and has good ideas, so maybe he's right. "It's possible she ran by when I was hiding. I heard a lot of footsteps, but couldn't see much," I say. It definitely *feels* like it could be true. Even if it's not. We have no way of truly knowing where Tinsley went.

We sit there for a few more minutes, trying to get up enough courage or energy or both to keep walking, especially now that it's pouring. The thunder seems to have died down, though, so hopefully the rain will end soon too. Eventually I stand up and hold a hand out to Leo. "Ready?"

He nods but doesn't take my hand. I think he might be a little angry at me, which is okay because I'm a little angry at me. I got them into this mess. We climb up over the muddy embankment, with Merlin and Little John right behind us. It's slippery, but I hold on to small trees to pull myself up. And then we head back to the creek and cross over. We're soaked to the skin now, so walking through the creek is no big deal. But I hear Mom's voice in my head again: *Keep your feet dry when you hike*. Though it's not like we have a choice now anyway. I really wanted to show her what I could do, but now my movie might just be something used in a missing person's case. *Ugh.* I have to stop thinking like that. Tinsley's fine, she's out there, I know it.

When we turn north, I tie a red scrap on a tree. We may have lost half our markers to get home, and Aaron and Michael might steal the rest, if they're stupid enough, but I have to try to mark our way as best as possible. This is all we've got.

We trudge through the muddy forest in silence for what feels like a very long time, but I think that's mostly because it feels like time has stopped. The rain has made everything so muggy, steam actually rises from the ground. My boots are caked with mud. I keep trying to push all the thoughts of everything Mom has taught me, and my failing to follow them, out of my head. But it's hard, and I can feel the threat of tears in the back of my throat. I need to focus, not let myself fold.

Other than the rain, and a few singing tree frogs, there are no other sounds. The dogs look like wet, dirty mops, but they don't seem to mind. They still chase each other every now and then, and once in a while Merlin will make a dash ahead like he's checking the way for us. Then he runs back to Leo and circles his legs for a scratch. At one point, though, he stops, lifts a paw, and stares straight ahead.

"What is it, boy?" Leo asks. The rain has quieted down, only a gentle pattering on leaves. We all stop and look ahead, but I don't see or hear anything.

Leo crouches down to be eye level with Merlin. "He senses something," Leo says. "But I don't see anyone."

"Tinsley!" I shout. "Tinsley, where are you?"

"That might not be the best idea," Leo says as he ducks. "What if it's the Sanderses?"

I bend down next to Leo. "She has to know we're trying to find her, though. She could be right ahead of us or behind us, and we'd never know because the trees are so dense."

"So could someone else."

"I don't know how else we'll find one another without calling out her name. We have to risk it." I pick up a new branch for a walking stick and then find one for Leo. "If we run into them again, they are not going to touch us," I say, shaking the stick.

Leo takes it. He doesn't look too sure about using it, if it comes to that, but he says, "Okay. We definitely can't keep running."

He's right. I never should have told us to take off like that. At the time it just seemed like we'd all run together, not in three different directions. But we'll find Tinsley soon and all of this will be behind me. Hopefully.

15

The next landmark symbol on the map is either a cave or a cliff, I think. As we walk, I keep my eyes open for anything remarkable that really stands out in the woods. Minutes turn into another hour and my stomach screams with hunger, but I don't want to stop now. It must be about two or three now. We're so quickly running out of time to find Tinsley, let alone the castle, before dark. I've even paused on filming anything for now because it just seems wrong.

By now, I'm sure all our parents are freaking out. Leo's mom probably called my dad, and they probably both called Tinsley's parents, and I'm sure it's a big giant mess. We're probably the talk of Newbridge. Talk about news! That's way better than dog poop! Dad might have even called Mom. She could be on a flight home. In the back of my mind, I've been hoping that if she came home this summer, it would be because I would tell her about all the cool things I was doing, and she wouldn't be able to stand missing out. But if she has to come home because she thinks I'm lost . . . my heart sinks again just thinking about it. She will not be happy about this reason, and I hate the thought of how worried she will be. It's possible they've even called the police and reported us *all* missing.

None of them have any idea we're here.

None of them can reach us because we have no cell service.

None of them have a clue we're missing a member of our party.

I feel like I'm going to throw up.

"Hey," Leo says. "Why are you stopping? Are you okay?"

I can't speak, only shake my head. Leo puts a hand on my back. "It's going to be okay, Lin."

"I have no idea how we're going to get home."

"We'll follow the fabric strips as far as we can, just as you planned."

"And when we get to where those boys took them down, then what?"

Leo doesn't say anything. Then he pipes up. "The compass, remember?"

I look at my muddy boots. "This was the wrong choice. We should have just gone home, like you said. Or tried to. We need help."

"And leave Tinsley *completely* alone up here? With the Sanderses and whoever else you saw? No. You were right. I was just scared, but we have to keep going, and we will find her. This is the best choice." Leo gives me a gentle push. I don't know if he believes what he's saying or not, but it works. "Come on. Keep moving. You're the leader of this expedition."

The thought chills me now. "You're not mad at me?" I ask as we forge ahead.

Leo hesitates, and says, "I was a little mad. But it's not your fault."

I step over a huge fallen tree, and hold a branch back so it doesn't smack Leo in the face. "I said we should run, that was foolish."

"We were all scared."

"We're going to be stuck out here another night," I say.

"Yeah," he says. Behind me I can hear him and the dogs trudging along.

"Our parents are probably losing their minds."

"My mom is probably trying to figure out how to contact the president right now."

I pause and look back at him. "I'm really sorry I got us into so much trouble."

"Honestly, other than the fact that Tinsley is missing, it's been totally worth it. Even if we don't find the castle."

I can't believe what I'm hearing. Leo's so quiet it's been hard to know if he's truly liked any of this or if he's just going along for the heck of it. "You mean it?"

"Climbing up the rock scramble, the views, the stars, and the deer? I know this is like small potatoes to what you're used to, but it's been amazing."

Leo saying that just made this big potatoes. I smile, though, and keep walking.

We come up along a sheer rock face in the hillside, almost

like it was built there for a purpose or fell out of the sky and lodged into the hill. It sticks out of the ground like a giant wedge. I look at the symbols on my arm and point out the one that looks like a harp shape, which I thought might be a cave, but now wonder if it's this wedge of rock. "You think this is that?"

"Might be," he says.

"We keep going north if it is, so we'll be on the right track regardless, but I think we're getting really close. The last symbol is this square with an X on it, though, which is odd."

"It reminds me of a barn door," Leo says.

"I can see that," I say. "Though a door in the woods doesn't make sense."

After a few more minutes of walking, Merlin does that thing with stopping and lifting his paw again. Leo puts a hand on my arm to stop me. "Someone is definitely up there. Look." He points through the trees, and sure enough there's someone walking way ahead of us. Someone with a long blond ponytail wearing big, professional, overnight backpacking equipment.

"I think it's a woman," I whisper. "You know what? Do you think it's that woman from the hardware store the other day?"

"Maybe," Leo says. "She's so far away it's hard to tell."

"If it is, she has to be looking for the castle, don't you think? So far off the trail like this? The lodge, the keys? Who the heck is she?"

Suddenly Merlin barks.

We duck and pull the dogs close to us.

"Shhhh!" Leo says to Merlin. "Enough."

"Do you think she saw us?" I ask, trying to see where she went.

"I don't know, but I'm sure she heard the barking."

We stay crouched for a minute, but the woman seems to have continued on her way, so we do the same. But then I realize there is a lot more at stake than the castle. Tinsley is still lost. We could really use this person's help. "Maybe she has a cell phone that works or radios or something. Maybe we should run up and tell her about Tinsley? She could help us look."

"You're right," Leo says. "Let's try to catch up to her."

I'm weirdly disappointed he agreed so quickly, because I'm afraid it will end our search, but at the same time, Tinsley is all alone and probably scared out of her mind. She's the priority now. We can't leave her, and we could definitely use some help. We jog through the woods to try to catch up to the other hiker, but she never comes into view again. Like Tinsley, she seems to have vanished.

It kind of freaks me out a little bit. "These woods are a little mysterious," I say. "I wonder if anyone has ever gone missing permanently up here." I regret saying it as soon as the words leave my mouth.

"Ugh, why would you say it like that?" Leo says. "Too creepy."

"Sorry," I say. "But people do go missing in national parks

now and then, like, one hundred percent vanish, with no trace."

"You're not making me feel any better."

"Some people think it's aliens." I'm like a runaway train now.

"Lin!"

"I'm just saying!" I snap my fingers. "Poof!"

Leo gives me a look like he's ready to knock me out with his walking stick.

"Sorry. I'm having hunger delusions," I say, laughing and then feeling badly for laughing. "The woods are actually one of the safest places you could be."

"Like I believe you now."

I cross my heart. "I promise."

The sun begins to peek through the canopy, sending small hazy rays of light between the leaves. It seems to illuminate a path through the trees, a fuzzy, glowing trail winding around branches and grape vines all leaning toward one another, almost forming an arch above us. A slight mist and warm musky smell rise up off the ferns and damp soil. The moss sparkles from raindrops. Suddenly it just feels like a magical place, like we've entered a completely new forest.

"This . . . is pretty cool," Leo says as he takes it all in.

I try to smile. It makes me happy to see him enjoy this, but inside I'm also so worried about Tinsley, it's hard to enjoy it too much.

We hit an area that has a huge incline and narrows, so that

we're almost walking on nothing more than an edge of rock as we make our way around the hill. The dogs masterfully balance right behind us. Ahead of me, I notice two small stone structures, sort of like the towers you see at the end of fancy driveways that sometimes have lion statues resting on top. "Leo, look!"

"Whoa," he says. "Looks like they're marking an entrance."

I'm afraid to get too excited, but I rush ahead to check it out. "Definitely marking an entrance. Come see!"

We walk down a short path and come into a clearing, or what maybe used to be a clearing. There are huge sections of stone walls, both standing and collapsed, with random trees growing through the piles.

"Are you thinking what I'm thinking?" I ask Leo.

He doesn't say anything, just looks at the destruction around us.

Everything is, or *was*, made out of stone, clearly a man-made structure, but now crumbled. A chimney still stands on the side like a soldier standing guard. There's one wall still up with a gaping hole for a window. Half of an arched doorway. It's very cool, but whatever it is, it's all in ruins.

"This can't be it," Leo says, but his voice sounds like he thinks it is.

I shake my head, but don't say anything. Because if *this* is it, if this is all that's left of Pen's Castle in the Clouds, then I *know* I made the worst decision of my life.

Now that the rain has stopped, the mosquitoes are out in full force. Sitting on a crumbled castle wall with Leo while we eat the remaining now soggy granola bars, we slap at the annoying biting bugs, and wonder where in the world Tinsley went, who the woman hiker is, and what happened to the Sanders brothers. This was the last way I was expecting this weekend to go. Even Dad is probably regretting sending me out to "explore" all the time. They will probably never trust me to do anything on my own ever again.

"Don't worry, Lin," Leo says. He bumps his shoulder into mine. But of course, him doing that makes me more upset. "Listen," he says. "We will finish this scrumptious meal, start the way back home, camp when we need to. We'll be home before you know it to get help."

"Leo, do you really think this is it?" I wave toward the piles of stone around us. "This can't be it."

"What else would it be?" He looks around. "I'm sorry it

didn't turn out the way we hoped, but we need to get help for Tinsley right away."

I nod and divide the rest of my granola bar and give it to the dogs. I should be starving, but I've actually lost my appetite completely, or maybe just got used to feeling hungry. "We should save one of these for Tinsley in case we run into her." I scratch my ankle where a mosquito got me and then hop off the wall. "I'm just going to look around a little bit, take some video before we go, okay?"

Leo nods. I can tell he feels really bad, but none of this is *his* fault. None of us thought the castle would be in ruins. The only person to blame for this is me. I remember once when my parents and I were out at a beautiful crystal-clear lake together, during one of Dad's breaks between homes, and we saw this guy doing flips off some giant boulders. It made Dad so nervous that he couldn't see whether or not the water was deep enough, even though he had no idea who the guy was. "There is a fine line between bravery and stupidity," he said to me. I didn't totally get what he meant at the time because I always thought being brave was good.

But now I realize what he was saying. I think I've definitely crossed that line.

Carefully, I wind around piles of stone and remaining walls of what must have been the interior of the castle. I turn on the camera and record some video of the ruins. In its own way, it's pretty spectacular. But the fact that I was expecting a majestic, hidden castle, like the one in Tinsley's photo, just makes the ruins seem worse. We're too late. From the looks of it, by decades. And now my movie has gone from an adventurous documentary of my summer to a tragic drama. Not what I was shooting for.

It will make for some cool footage, though, this abandoned, crumbled castle, hidden in the woods. I can imagine what it used to look like in its glory. Maybe I can make up a story around it, fictionalize my movie instead. I sigh, angry with myself for even worrying about this right now, and almost turn off the camera, but then I notice some graffiti on a wall, which is strange considering no one was supposed to have found this place before.

I aim the camera on the writing:

BRAD WUZ HERE '98
JM + JR 4EVA

A few more steps and there's a bunch of charred glass and beer cans with bullet holes in them around an old campfire ring. *Strange.* Then a few more steps and a pair of sneakers sticking out from under a stony shelf. I peek partway under.

The sneakers are attached to feet and legs with one red sock and one green.

I scream like I've never screamed before.

All at once, the dogs and Leo rush over to me, and the pair

of legs moves. I jump back at first, but quickly realize who they belong to.

"Tinsley!" I yell, and basically jump on her, hugging her tight as I can. "I thought we'd never find you. I've been so worried." Leo comes up and hugs us both. Merlin and Little John circle us and bark.

"Where did you go?" I ask when I finally let her go. Her face is a filthy mess, with a few scratches. I realize her clothes are in about the same state. "Are you okay?"

She nods, a little breathless, but smiles. "Yes, I'm totally fine. I ran for my life when you said to! This is where I ended up, and when it started raining I crawled under there to try to stay dry. I guess I fell asleep for a while."

I've never felt so relieved in my life. I almost start crying, but instead just hug her again.

"Where were you two?" she asks.

"We ran, but we both stopped and then found each other after the Sanderses disappeared. Lin was afraid you were abducted by aliens," Leo says.

"Lin, *you* believe in aliens?" Tinsley asks, very excited about the prospect. "Now, that would have been an adventure! So shall we continue up to . . . ?" She trails off like she's said a little bit more than she meant to.

We wait for her to finish, but she doesn't. She kicks around some leaves as though looking for something she dropped. Leo slaps the back of his neck, and I catch a glimpse of the symbols on his arm, realizing the Tetris-looking symbol must have meant these ruins. Tinsley must have figured that out, and that's why she stopped here. She has to know more than she's told me. Now I have to ask.

"Tinsley, why do you have a picture of the castle in your backpack?"

She seems to be considering an answer for a few seconds, and finally throws her hands out and talks really fast. "It was my grandfather's. Either he took it or a friend did. We don't really know, it's just been in the family for a long time." She sighs loudly. "Finally got that off my chest. I should have told you from day one."

"Why didn't you?" I ask.

"I don't know. I thought I could just be helpful and not mention it. I had an idea of where the castle would be positioned on the mountain, because of the picture and some of the things my dad has said, just no idea how to get that far. I needed you for that, Lin. I never would have known where to start or be brave enough to go alone. But we both wanted the same thing—to find the castle."

I'm stunned to silence, which doesn't happen much. Tinsley used me?

"So your grandfather's already been there?" Leo asks, looking back and forth between me and Tinsley.

Tinsley crosses her arms around her middle, like a self-hug. Her eyes get glassy. "I don't know for sure. All I know is my dad and his dad and probably his dad before him have been talking about that castle *forever*. And I never had any idea why because as far as I know, none of them ever actually tried to find it."

Everything from the day bubbles up in my chest. The photo, the rain, the Sanders boys, Tinsley being lost for hours, the roller coaster of thinking we found the castle all crumbled. Even though I try, I can't keep myself from shouting. "So you used me to find it? What were you going to do once we got there? Claim it for yourself? After all the work I've put into this?"

Tinsley looks shocked.

"You're not the only one who put work in, Lin," Leo says quietly, which stings.

"I put in the most," I say. Even though I'm not sure that's true, it's felt like it.

"We've all done the work," Leo says. "Yes, you know more about being out here and directions and all that, but we've all carried the food, made decisions. We got into the Freemasons' building together, searched at the library together. You're not doing this alone, you know?"

"I don't want us to fight," Tinsley says. She comes over to me and grabs my hand. "I promise you. I wanted us to find it *together*, claim it *together*. And I don't like talking about my dad—it makes me too sad—so I didn't get into all of it."

I know she's telling the truth because of how many times she'd change the subject whenever anything got serious. I believe her, but there's part of me that still feels tricked. Although now I'm not sure if it was Tinsley who tricked me or just that I fooled myself into thinking I was doing this alone.

"Dad always said 'someday' he'd have the time to go up and look for himself, but he never has, and now? Well, anyway, that's why I wanted to go with you and—" Her voice cracks. "Maybe find it for him. But not to claim it for myself. He'd be proud of me no matter what."

This whole time Tinsley's dad has been trying to recover, and I don't even know how long he's been hurt or how bad. I have no idea what the future holds for him, or their family—I never even asked. No wonder she wanted to find it for him so badly. It suddenly occurs to me that she's not home to even help her mom like she usually does. She gave up a lot to be here. I didn't give up anything, I just steamrolled ahead.

"He's still going to be proud of you," I say. "We're going to find it."

Tinsley tries to smile through her tears. "I only brought the photo in case we got lost and it might help somehow. I had to sneak it out of my dad's office in the middle of the night."

"Wow," I say. "That's really sweet of you. Although I feel kind of stupid now." This whole time, even though we'd set out *together*, I'd truly only been thinking of this being my discovery. My quest. My responsibility. But this is about more than just me.

"Leo, I'm sorry. I know we've all done a ton of work."

"It's fine," he says.

"Don't feel stupid!" Tinsley says. "You—we—still get to be the ones to truly discover it."

"But you kind of already know where it is?"

"Not exactly. I know we have to keep climbing up to the top of the mountain, which is why I knew this wasn't the castle. Looking closely at the picture you can tell it's too far down. I have no idea where it is once you get up there. And I had no idea where to start, which is why I've never explored myself. That and the immense fear of bears."

"So far that hasn't come true, thank god," says Leo. "But I think Merlin and Little John would have scared them away. Lin says they don't like noise."

I smile, proud he remembers my text lesson. I look at them both and ask, "So are we all still in for this? Because we're going to be stuck out here another night at this point."

"I'm not ready to give up," Tinsley says.

"Me neither." Leo puts a hand out. "One for all—"

My heart leaps. Tinsley and I each put our hand on his and say, "All for one!"

We throw our hands up in the air and start gathering our things. I'm so relieved to know the truth about the photo, but now I'm worried about the fact that our stuff is soaked, including what's left of our food, and I consider our options for camping again. But I don't get the chance to mention any of this because suddenly the woman with the cargo pants and long blond ponytail is standing right in front of us. Even the dogs didn't hear her.

"Well, now, I was wondering when we all might finally bump into one another," she says, and holds up a bundle of fish. "Who's hungry?" Then she slips out of her giant backpack, lets it down to the ground, and begins to set up a camp. "Anna Joy Pace," she says, which just feels so crazy coincidental to Annie Smith Peck that I'm immediately enchanted with every word she has to say. And now that she's up close again, I'm certain she was the woman in the hardware store that day. Which means she has Tinsley's dad's keys.

She tells us she caught a few small trout in the creek, which is where I first saw her, and when she heard the dogs barking, she knew she wasn't in the woods alone. But she doesn't ask us why we're here.

"Everyone calls me AJ," she says. "So you might as well too. When I came across these ruins, they just seemed like the best place to fry up some fish and camp for the night. So what do you say?" she says. "Join me for dinner?"

"Are you . . . going to ask us why three kids are in the woods alone?" Leo asks. I think we're all wondering the same thing, but I get the feeling she doesn't really care. Not in a bad way, though. More like she just doesn't know kids being alone in the woods is not normal.

AJ shrugs. "I figured you're on a campout. What else would you be doing?" She doesn't seem to think it's strange at all and begins to build a nice campfire ring. Then she pauses and looks up. "You're not all running away from home or something, are you? Because I'd have to draw the line there. I won't be an accomplice to that."

"Oh, no, nothing like that," I say quickly. "We're just . . . on a campout, like you said. But we got a little lost in the rain."

"People looking for ya?"

"Maybe?"

She looks me directly in the eyes.

"Probably," I say. "Do you happen to have a working cell phone?"

AJ shakes her head. "I don't use those things." She taps her forehead. "I depend on this."

I probably shouldn't be relieved, but I am. I'm not ready to go home yet, even though I know Dad is probably so upset. Now that we have food, can dry off by the fire, and finish searching in the morning, I'm more energized than ever. I know finding the castle will be worth it *for all of us*, and Dad will have to understand why we did it after he sees it. At least I hope.

"Why are you up here?" I ask. "I mean, hiking off the trail."

"Just doing a little exploring. I've hiked most of the great trails in the country, and I've done the AT twice, so I wanted to see some new areas of the mountain." She pulls a knife out of one of her pants' many pockets. On a flat stone, a little bit away from us, she chops off the fish head, and then guts and cleans it. "Make sure that fire gets real hot!" Then she works on the next one.

We're all a little shocked at how easily she uses that knife.

She talks a little about her times hiking the AT, and it reminds me of the times Mom and I would meet other hikers. AJ is the kind of person my parents would totally hang out with, like a lot of other travelers we've met on the road. Makes me miss my mom a little bit, but mostly I just soak up everything she says and can't wait to tell them later.

"Do you think she's telling the truth?" Leo whispers to me as we gather extra kindling.

"I don't know," I say. "Not the whole truth. I'm positive she's the woman who caught us at the lodge, though. Don't you think she sounds the same?"

Tinsley nods. "I wouldn't forget that voice."

AJ has to be heading toward the castle, I think. "No matter what happens tonight, our plan should be to wake up extra early and start off before she gets up," I say. "And hope we get there first."

AJ joins us back around the fire. She places three large green sticks across the pit and lays the fish across them. They begin to cook from the hot coals immediately. "Normally I just eat peanut butter and oatmeal and dried jerky when I'm out here. But got real lucky this time."

The way she talks makes it sound like she lives in the woods. She's like a real survivalist. "Do you have a . . . home?" I ask.

"Yeah, sorta," she says. "But I'm not there much. I prefer to travel by foot."

"Don't you have a job?" Leo asks. "I mean, you have to work somehow, right?"

"I'm between jobs right now," AJ says as she turns the fish carefully with a metal fork she had in her canteen. "Which is why I'm traveling. I was out west for a while searching for the Forrest Fenn treasure. You ever heard of it?"

We all shake our heads no.

"I tend to get caught up in treasure hunts, legends, stuff that no normal person has the time, or mind, to do." She laughs. "Fenn was some old rich dude who hid something up in the Rocky Mountains somewhere. He wrote a whole book about it, and tons of people have tried to find it over the years. I was out there for about two months when it came out that someone beat me to it."

"Two months in the woods?" Tinsley nearly squeaks. "How did you carry enough food and water?"

"I can carry quite a bit," AJ says with a smirk. "I'm a bit more seasoned than you, Pinkie. Plus, for water, I carry these." She reaches in her bag and pulls out a few blue tubes. "Magic straws. You can use them to drink from any natural moving water source." She hands one to Tinsley. "You can keep it. Don't drink from puddles."

Tinsley looks awed as she examines the tube.

"So, it was real?" I interrupt. "Like he put actual treasure in the woods?"

AJ nods. "Don't know what it was exactly, but it was supposed to be worth a million bucks. I thought if I found it, it would allow me to keep traveling for a very long time. But this time I lost."

Tinsley's mouth drops open. "That's amazing that someone would just hide a million dollars in the woods for other people to find."

"Even more amazing that people think it's real," Leo

mumbles. "I mean, it sounds like fun, but how do you know it was actually there?"

AJ looks at him, puzzled. "Well, it was found, so it must have been."

"But you didn't know that while you were searching."

She shrugs. "Doesn't matter. I hoped it was. And, honestly, even though I didn't get there first, the search was still worth it. When you're out in the wilderness like that, surviving on your own, it's pretty amazing."

Leo looks at me and back at AJ. "I know someone else who would say that."

AJ pulls all the fish off and places them on a cloth napkin she has. "Okay, help yourself. But be careful. They can be bony."

We take what we want and give each of the dogs some as well. It's hard to not gobble it down, and I don't even like fish. We're so hungry it doesn't matter. We eat until all of it is gone, and we're licking our fingers even though there is not a flake left to be seen. We share the last of the marshmallows with AJ, even though they are a bit sticky, and wash it all down with a lemonade she makes for us with a sugary powder in her supplies. We tell her all about the Sanderses and how they might still be up here. She has a glint of recognition in her eyes when Leo tells her their names. I don't say anything, but I definitely notice.

As we lounge around the fire, AJ tells us about a lot of her adventures and some of the people she's run into on the trails, some friendly and willing to share supplies or fire, others not so much. "Overall, most of my experiences have been positive," she says.

Eventually, Leo and Tinsley drift off, snuggling with the dogs, but I'm so captivated by AJ's stories, even their snoring doesn't distract me.

"Never let anyone tell you that you can't travel alone just because you're a girl. You have to be smart, do your research about the trails and what to bring, and stay safe, but any of you could do it. Well, obviously you already are."

"You remind me of a younger version of my mom," I say through a yawn, sort of absentmindedly. I didn't mean to bring up my parents. I was enjoying AJ talking to me like she happened to run into me on a trail, her stories of places she's been and things she's learned. Talking to me like I'm just like her.

"She a backpacker?"

"She's an . . . everything."

AJ smiles. "Is she why you're up here on this camping trip alone? Tryna be like her?"

My face flushes; I didn't think I was that obvious. "I'm just searching for something, sort of like a treasure, I guess. I wanted to be the first to find it, to show her I could be like her. Maybe . . ." I trail off.

"Maybe better?" AJ suggests. "There's no shame in it. Your mother sounds like an inspiring person, and she's raised up a brave, independent daughter. My kind of mom. I hope you're using everything she's taught you."

"I'm trying," I say, although secretly leaving home is definitely not something she'd be proud of. "I'm not sure I *can* do this without her, though. I'm not sure I'll be the first."

"Well, I doubt your mom is going to love you any less if it doesn't work out. Can I ask you something, though?"

I yawn again. "Yeah."

She folds her hands in her lap and leans toward the flames a little bit. "Why do you need to be the first? Is a discovery less important if more than one person discovers it? You think every person who lands on the moon is going to be disappointed because someone else already did it?"

I stare at her through the flames and say nothing. She winks at me, lies back, and puts an arm over her face, and I assume that's the end of her talk.

It's an awesome night overall. But when I lie back on my sleeping bag, something in the way she said all that makes me think she knows exactly what we're looking for. Considering the lodge and the key and this conversation, it makes the decision to leave early even easier, because it's clear AJ is searching for something here on the mountain, just like she has on many other mountains. I'm willing to bet my life it's the castle.

And as much as I like her, despite what she said, I still want the three of us to find it on our own.

17

It's not even dawn when I gently shake Leo awake. He moans a complaint, but I cover his mouth. "Shhhhh," I whisper in his ear. "It's me. Come on. We're going to get an early start."

He sits up and rubs his eyes. What's left of the fire, just a small flicker, lights up his face, illuminating creases on his cheek. "This isn't early. It's the middle of the night."

"I know. Just trust me, okay? We have to go now." I crawl over to Tinsley, and she's already awake.

"Got it," she whispers, holding up a palm to my face. I guess neither of them are morning people. The moon is still brilliant, but the sky is brightening way in the distance, and it will only take minutes for the sun to be high enough to light up the woods. By then, we will be out of sight of the ruins, and AJ. It makes me a little sad to sneak off like this, but I want us to find the castle as soon as possible.

We try to be as quiet as we can, but it's difficult to roll up sleeping bags without making any noise. Plus, a lighter load will make the rest of the climb easier. In the end I decide we will leave them and pick them up on the way back. We will be getting home today, anyway, so if all goes well we won't need them again. Merlin and Little John shake off sleep, wag their tails, and follow right in step as we leave camp and head for the highest point of the mountain, Kittatinny Peak.

Once we are far enough away, I apologize for surprising them so early. "I just got a bad feeling last night that AJ is also heading for the castle. It's too coincidental that she's off the trail in the same area. Which is why I figured we get up at a ridiculous time and just start walking."

"I wondered what you were thinking last night when she said that," Leo says. "I think I fell asleep in the middle of that conversation."

"You both did," I say. "But you didn't miss much. She told me a lot of hiking stories." I don't mention the *being first* part, mostly because I'm still wrapping my own brain around it.

"Have either of you thought about what happened to the Sanderses?" he asks. "Do you think they found their way home?"

"I think they're probably too stupid to find their way home," I say. Then I feel really bad for saying it. Especially since I'm not even sure yet how we're going to find our way home without AJ's help. They didn't have any supplies with them that I saw. Following us was not the smartest thing for them to do, but we're not responsible for them. "But really, I don't know, hopefully they did."

"I'm not going to lie, at first I kept picturing them out

there, eaten half to death by mosquitoes, starving, soaking wet," Leo says. "But now? Yeah, I hope they got home."

"I don't like them, but it would be pretty awful if they were lost, lost," Tinsley says. "I mean, aren't either one of you a little scared? Like, for us?"

I am a little scared, but I try not to think about it too much, and I don't want them to get too worried. "Maybe a little," I finally say. "But I'm more focused on the castle. We still have a bit of almond butter left to share. We'll find it today, get our videos, and get back home. I can feel it."

"If we don't find it by, like, noon," Leo says, "I vote we head home. If nothing else, the dogs have to eat and rest. It's probably going to take some time to get back down."

"I agree," Tinsley says. "What do you think, Lin?"

"I think we better walk faster."

And we do. We trudge hard up the narrow ledge of the hillside using every bit of strength we have left, which is not much. Slipping in our sneakers, tripping over roots, sweating in the sun by the time it's shining bright. I smell like an old gym bag. Noon is quickly approaching when we run into a sheer rock face similar to the last one we saw, only this one is blocking the rest of the way up the mountain. And it's at least fifty feet tall; there's no way around it. A complete dead end. I press my hands on the surface, feeling around for footholds or little ledges that might help pull me up.

"I am not climbing that," Tinsley says. She takes a step back, looks all the way up, and shakes her head. "Yeah. Nope."

"We must have interpreted the symbols wrong," Leo says. "The last one is this square. But the symbol for that first rock face was different, remember." He looks at me with an apologetic expression. "I'm sorry, Lin, I think we messed up."

I chew on the inside of my cheek a little bit, shake my head. Look at them, look at the rock wall. I pace the length of it searching for clues. "No. No, everything made sense so far. Everything we were looking for showed up."

"Random things that exist in the woods showed up. I mean, we could have interpreted anything to be anything and it would have shown up eventually," he says.

"We can't come this far to stop because of a dumb rock wall," I say. "There has to be a way up to the top of the mountain."

Leo sits down on a small flat rock. "Look around! There's nothing else. We'd have to walk halfway back down to get around this thing and go up a different way."

"Then let's try that."

Tinsley drops her head. "No more, Lin. We have to go back. We can make plans to come again. Now that we know some of the way, it will be so much faster! We won't get chased or lost or wet."

Deep down I get a rush of that frustrating feeling, like other people are making decisions for me. Like when Mom and Dad make me feel like a yo-yo. "What the heck? You're both against me?"

"We're not against you. We're just going to be in so much

trouble as it is," Leo says. "Everyone is going to be so worried. Plus we're out of food. Now this?"

"I seriously can't walk anymore, Lin," Tinsley says, dropping her head back. "I feel like Dorothy lost in the poppy fields in Oz about to faint amongst the petals!"

"Hang in a little longer for me, Dorothy, okay? We can figure this out." We have to. I can't go home without proof of the castle now and get in trouble all for nothing. The only thing I'll prove is that I can't do what I set out to do. "And it's not noon, Leo. You said by noon."

"I did." He points up to the sky, where the sun is very close to being right overhead. "But that's almost now." He sits on a large stone and scratches his hair, which is getting a little greasy. Tinsley lies down on a fallen tree, which can't be at all comfortable, her arm draped over her face, and the dogs lie in the dirt. Everyone is dirty, tired, and hungry. I'm sure I look just as much of a mess. But I'm not quitting yet.

I turn my back on them and study the wall. One of the things Annie Smith Peck said in that book Mom got me was "Climbing is hard . . . the only real pleasure is the satisfaction of going where no man has gone before and few can follow." But AJ said you don't have to be first to enjoy a discovery. And Mom says to always trust my gut.

I don't agree with Leo. I think we solved the symbols perfectly. This wall has to be what the symbol of the square with the X on it meant, the one Leo said looked like a barn door. But that would mean other than the castle builder, everyone has been stopped by this rock. And we know that can't be true or there would be no legend, no carvings on the boulder, and in fact, it would be impossible to build the castle in the first place, if one had to haul all the supplies over this wall. So there must be a way *through*.

"Look for a door!" My shouting startles all of them. "I'm serious! Look for a door."

"Lin, it's solid rock," Tinsley says from under her arm. "There's not going to be a door."

"Yes, there is. Leo, you thought the symbol looked like a door and I think you're right. Think about it, it's like the sword in the stone! Only it's the 'door' in the stone!" I say, trying to make a joke to get them up again.

They look at me for a minute. Leo scratches his head. Tinsley kicks at the dirt. "Okay," she says. I can tell they don't believe a word I'm saying, but they get up and help me look anyway.

I press as hard as I can in all different spots across the wall. Nothing budges. "In your picture, Tinsley, the castle is on the ridge overlooking the river, which means it's facing west. It has to be on this side of the ridge. If we went up a different way, we wouldn't find it."

"That part makes sense," she says. "I just can't see how a door in solid rock makes sense."

We all stand back a bit and stare at the wall some more. And that's when I see it. All the way over on the right side against the hill, there is a corner of something carved on the rock. Just a tiny bit of it is exposed out of the dirt. I run over and dig the dirt away from the rock as fast as I can. Tinsley and Leo join me, and then the dogs even dig with us, although they don't dig in the right spot, they just dig. We grab sticks to help move soil, and soon there's much more than carvings. There's an entire mechanism buried underground. We've uncovered part of some kind of lever-and-gear system.

"Can you move that handle?" Leo asks.

"Not yet. This must have gotten buried over the years. I wish we had shovels!"

We keep digging as fast as we can. My fingers are nearly black with dirt and a little bloodied from catching the corners of stones and roots. I use the flat side of a rock like a chisel to help break apart packed dirt. Eventually we dig into the ground far enough I can grab the lever with both hands. I push on it as hard as I can. "You have to help. It's totally rusted."

All three of us put all our weight into it. Slowly it jerks downward, little movements at a time. "We're doing it!" I shout. Then there's an *awful* scraping sound like the loudest fingernails-on-chalkboard screech ever.

Tinsley jumps and yelps. "Look!" She points to the other side of the wall, where we now see a huge slab of rock has moved slightly out of place. "It *is* a door in the stone! Keep going!" She sits on the lever, and we laugh, but it totally works. The secret door slides open, a secret door that hasn't been opened for maybe a hundred years or more.

And we get to walk through it.

PART THREE

18

It's very dark inside, like a cave. In fact, that's exactly what it seems it used to be: a small old cave someone used as a tunnel and blocked with a perfectly hand-cut rock. It's damp and silent. The walls are very close to us, and we have to squish together to all fit. Leo keeps his flashlight ahead for us as we walk.

"I really don't want to run into any bats or bears," Tinsley says. She walks right next to me, hanging on one arm and shining her own flashlight on the dripping, cobwebby walls. We don't see any signs of life, however, other than some beetles and a few spiders.

"Too small for bears," I say.

"But not bats?" she asks.

I don't answer.

"Look," Leo says. "There's a tiny bit of light up there."

Sure enough, there is a pinprick of light from an opening that when we reach it is not big enough for us to get out. I'm sure it's been covered over the years, like the door mechanism.

"We're going to have to dig some more," I say.

Fortunately, this proves much easier than the door. We break the wall apart. Stones fall at our feet and at one point smash Tinsley's foot. "Ow!" she howls, and hops back. "That did not feel good."

"Are you okay?" I say. "Can you walk on it?" I bend down to look, as if that's going to help. "Do you think anything's broken?"

"I think it's okay," she says, and rolls her ankle a little bit and tests out her foot. She says it's fine, and we give the stones one last push, away from us, finally opening up the closed exit. We step out into the bright sun again. My eyes take a minute to adjust and look around. It's as though the woods have completely disappeared.

We're in an overgrown but obvious courtyard of a nearly perfectly preserved castle, surrounding us on all sides.

"The wall was part of the building?" Leo looks back. "Wow. It looked like any other rock face in the woods! You'd never know!"

"I think that was the point," I say, looking around and taking it all in. I turn the camera on immediately. "Can you even believe this?"

We are surrounded by high stone walls, wildly covered in ivy and vines. In the middle of the courtyard, there are stone arches and garden gates also overgrown with grape vines and prickly rosebushes. A massive fountain sits in the middle of the garden, cracked and slightly lopsided. It's like we've walked into a forgotten fairy tale.

Birds fly overhead, a few land on the walls, a couple fly in glassless windows, and I think about how to them, this is no big deal. They probably see it every day, build nests in the rafters, fly in and out like it's any other part of the mountain. The castle has clearly been claimed by nature, even though it's still in incredible shape. A few small trees, high grasses, and wildflowers fill the courtyard. On one side of the main tower, moss has grown all the way up and onto the roof like a beautiful spring-green blanket. The windows are all too high for us to reach. A pair of wooden doors at the base of the main tower seem to be the only way inside the fortress.

Unless you're a bird.

I look at Leo and Tinsley. Maybe I was wrong. Maybe I'm not a fish in a tree full of birds. Maybe I'm a bird too, and I just had to find the right flock.

I lower the camera. "You guys. You're my flock."

Leo laughs. "Your what?"

My face burns a little bit, but I say, "I just mean I'm so glad we found this *together*." I hold my arms out wide and slowly spin. "*We* found it. Pen's Castle in the Clouds! The three of us. Together. Just look at it!"

Tinsley claps and bounces on her feet. She grabs me by the shoulders. "We did it!"

"Well, let's stop dancing around and go in!" Leo says. "You need inside footage too!"

"Yes!" I say. "We have a legend to document!" Leo and Tinsley nod, still gaping at the sights. They head toward the big wooden doors while I record them. Leo tries to open them, but they don't move. "Tins, give me a hand here!"

"It's going to be really dark in there," Tinsley says as she slightly limps over. I guess that rock hit her foot harder than she let on. "I'm not a fan of all this dark."

"It won't all be dark. Once we get inside the main part of the building there are some windows. And we have our flashlights still," Leo says. "Are you all right?"

"Yeah," she says. "It's not too bad, just sore." She rolls her foot around. "Between twisting my ankle on the first day and this, I'm bound to lose a whole leg next."

"Just be careful," he says. Together they pull the door open, which I capture on video. It's a perfect shot. A couple of birds fly out. Then I turn off the camera and help them the rest of the way with the heavy doors so we can get inside.

The tower is empty, but we find a set of spiral stairs that takes us into the main part of the building. There's not much inside other than fireplaces in every room, ornate woodwork panels, and a lot of stone and materials for building. No furniture or any personal belongings. It seems the castle was never finished.

"I don't think anyone ever lived here," I say. "This is all masonry supplies."

"That's kind of sad," Tinsley says. "This huge home standing empty all this time, and no one to enjoy it." She glances at me. "Imagine what our dads could do with this," she whispers. "If only mine was in better shape. Can you imagine living in a castle?"

I actually can. But even if my dad could fix this place up, we never live in the places he works on. We always keep moving on to the next project, which I have always loved. It surprises me that there's suddenly a tug in my heart to stay put. Not necessarily in the castle. But nearby, not moving. Maybe for a while.

We walk into an enormous wood-paneled room that seems like it could be a ballroom or massive dining room. The boards squeak beneath our feet as we walk.

"I *love* this place," Tinsley says dreamily. "I feel like I'm in *Beauty and the Beast*!" Her voice sounds hollow in the vast space. She walks out into the center, holds her arms as if she's dancing with a partner, and starts humming a tune.

"Or *Camelot*," Leo adds. I hadn't even noticed he pulled his book out of the bag. He shows me an illustration that looks remarkably like the castle we're standing in.

"So you think that part of the legend is true also? That this has something to do with King Arthur?"

He shrugs and closes the book. "I mean, maybe it was just built by someone who loved the story, but it's an interesting coincidence."

"Come on, you guys!" Tinsley waves to us. "Dance with me!"

Leo looks a little hesitant, but we both join her, all three of us dancing with invisible partners in the center of a giant dance floor. Tinsley hums something lively and dances like a ballerina. We spin, and laugh, and Leo pretends to dip his date low to the floor and then flip her back up.

"Don't try that for real," I tease. "You'll send her flying across the room!"

"Here, put everything down," Tinsley says, which we do, and then she makes Leo and me hold hands. "Let me teach you a real dance."

"I can't real dance," Leo says, dropping my hands.

"Just try?" she asks. "Give it a chance. It's a waltz. No better dance than a waltz in a ballroom!"

Leo rolls his eyes but takes my hands again.

"One hand goes on Lin's waist," Tinsley says. Leo obliges. Tinsley holds her arms out and starts counting, "One, two, three, one, two, three . . ." She steps forward, to the side, and back again, and it's a lot to keep track of. But then she holds on to us and sort of guides us through the steps at the same time, while humming. "See! Hold this arm up. Good, Leo! Now take your steps on the count. It's easy!" Even Merlin and Little John seem excited by the dancing, and circle us, tails wagging the entire time.

"How did you learn to dance like this?" I ask.

"YouTube. I learned all the formal dances on there. You have to be a triple threat in show business. Acting, singing, and dancing."

"I'll show you a triple threat." Leo grabs my hands tighter, holds me out, and we spin and spin and spin as fast as we can until I'm screaming with laughter. Tinsley claps and skips around us. We're all having so much fun and laughing so hard that when Leo accidently lets go of me and I fall back, the abrupt loud *Craaack* doesn't quite make sense.

It all happens so fast. I feel myself plummet. Heat and pain sear through my legs at the same time. My feet go right through the floor, which instantly tears my legs up. I scream, fearing sure death in a bottomless pit, but instead quickly come to a jolting halt. The hole is too small for my whole body to fall through, so I'm left hanging with my legs dangling into the room below us. It's like I've fallen through ice, and I grasp for anything on the floor to hold me there.

"Lin!" both Tinsley and Leo scream.

Leo instructs Tinsley to lie flat on the floor, and they each grab one of my hands, just like you would if you were on thin ice. The floor holds, and with their help, I'm able to pull myself out and get back up. They rush me to the side of the room, far from the hole, and we lean up against the wall.

"Are you okay?" Leo asks. He examines my legs, which are a splintered, bloody mess, my jeans all tattered. If I'd been wearing shorts it would have been way worse. "Oh man, you are all torn up." He runs over to where we dropped our bags and searches through for something. "Did either of you bring extra clothes?"

Tinsley shakes her head. I don't have anything either, and

of course we left our sleeping bags behind, so we don't even have them. "And you thought *you* were going to lose a leg, Tinsley," I say, trying to laugh. I carefully pull a few small splinters out of my calf and knee. Leo takes his shirt off and starts tearing it to shreds.

"What are you doing?" I ask.

"You have to wrap some of those cuts," he says. "That one is bad." He takes a long strip of his shirt and ties it around my leg, and then repeats it for two other larger scrapes. It hurts, but the pressure from the bandage helps. Blood seeps through at first, then seems to stop after a few seconds. When he's done, he leans his head against the wall. His face is pale.

"Thank you, Leo." I put my hand on his. He nods and flips his hand around and squeezes mine before he lets go.

"Wow," Tinsley says. "Good thinking. You're a hero!"

"Yeah," I say. "You saved my life."

Leo shakes his head. "No, just the smart thing to do. With a mom who's a nurse, you just learn this stuff." He takes the last bit of shirt he has left and ties it around his head like a headband.

"Nice look," I say.

"I never should have spun you like that."

"You didn't know the floor was going to give out."

"Are you okay? Can you walk?" he asks.

I get up and test out my legs. "Yeah, they're fine. Just shredded a bit." I laugh even though the thought does make me a little queasy. I'm lucky all I got was splinters and cuts. I could have been killed. Goose bumps immediately rise up on my arms. "That was close."

"That could have been really bad," Leo says. "I think we should stick to the courtyard."

"Yeah," I say. "You're right."

We gather up our things and make our way back toward the stairs that go through the tower, but pause to look out a window over the valley before we descend back into darkness. The view is amazing—rolling green hills, the river snaking way down below us, birds dipping on wind currents in the valleys. The drop from the castle on this side is actually a little frightening. I can only imagine what the three of us look like, hanging out the window, if a plane flew by now. All three of us have filthy hands and faces, Leo with no shirt and a T-shirt headband. We must look like we were raised by wolves.

"This really has been incredible, don't you think?" I ask. "I kind of don't want to leave."

"We can come here whenever we want," Tinsley says. "Now that we know the way, we can prepare better and it won't take as long."

"But now that we've completely dug out the door, other people are going to find it," Leo says.

"That's true," I agree. "And Tinsley, what do you think your dad and the Freemasons will say?"

Tinsley tilts her head a little bit, doesn't look at me. "I've been thinking about that. I'm not sure. I guess it depends on whether or not they *truly* knew the castle was here and were keeping it secret, or if they were only guarding the legend and also hoping to be the ones to find it one day." She looks a little sad.

"You okay?" I ask.

Her face gets a little cloudy, like she's lost in thought somewhere. "I, um . . . I was just thinking what it would be like if he were here right now."

I totally understand because there's part of me that wishes my parents were here too. But the other part of me is proud we were the ones to do it by ourselves. I put an arm around her. "You'll have such a great story to tell him. And you can show him all the photos and video I took."

"He's going to love it."

"My parents too. Once they're done being mad," I say.

"Honestly, I don't think my mom will care about the castle," Leo says. "She'll be upset about me being missing and dirty. That's all that matters to her."

"I know we're going to be in a lot of trouble," I say. "We can tell everyone it was all my idea."

"No way. Don't say that!" Leo says. "I didn't have to go along with it. It was time for me to stand up to her. I mean, it didn't have to be quite so drastic, but she has to stop trying to keep me in a bubble forever. Maybe once she gets over being mad, this will actually show her I'm fine on my own."

"Do you really feel that way now?" I ask. "That you're okay on your own?"

"I think so," he says. "Although I don't really mean by myself, just that she doesn't need to be as worried as she is."

"I hope she gets it, Leo." I put my other arm over one of his shoulders. We stand like that for several minutes. I don't think any of us are ready to go, no matter what is waiting for us back home.

There's just one thing that doesn't make total sense to me. "You know, I've been thinking," I say. "It's a beautiful castle, but why has it been so hard to find? And why are the Freemasons so secretive, even if it was built by a descendant of King Arthur? I don't get it. It's just a building."

"Unless there's something else here," Tinsley suggests. "Something hidden in the castle that is worth something?"

"From what we saw, it seems like it's mostly just a giant, empty castle," Leo says.

"But we didn't go in all the rooms," I say. "Tinsley might be right. And maybe it's like what AJ was talking about—that old guy who hid treasure in the Rocky Mountains. Maybe someone hid something here a long time ago. Something only the Freemasons know about, and that's what they've truly been guarding." Now I definitely don't want to leave yet. Not before we check every corner. We're all already going to be in so much trouble. What's another hour? "What do you say we do one quick search before we leave?"

"Do I have to remind you that you just almost fell into an abyss?" Leo asks. "Not worth the risk."

"If we stay to the outer walls, we should be fine. We were dancing and jumping around and that caused too much stress, but near the walls the floor will be stronger," I say. It sounds like it could be true, like something my dad might say, and even though I am nervous about walking around in there, I feel like we have to. We've come this far.

But suddenly there are some voices and shouting from the courtyard. We duck and crawl over to the other side of the room to peek out a window that overlooks the yard. Aaron, Michael, and Seth all stand there, gaping.

"This can't be happening," I whisper. I sit down with my back against the wall, and Leo and Tinsley join me. "The only way out is back into the yard. We're totally trapped."

"You know they're going to come up here," Tinsley says. "We have to move."

"They do not get to claim this," I say. "Or anything else that might be here."

"We'll hide, and after they leave, try to beat them home," she says. "What other choice do we have?"

"Fight them," Leo says.

Tinsley and I look at him and both say, "What?"

He's completely serious. "That's the other choice we have. I know we can't win an actual fight, but I've run and hidden too many times. I have to face them. Or this will never end."

We make our way deeper into the castle, as far as we can go, quietly searching for anything to defend ourselves with. Like the first few rooms, most are empty except for leaves and twigs, abandoned birds' nests, cobwebs, and dust. Piles of unused blocks of stone everywhere. Nothing that would keep any of those boys away from us. But then we come into an area that seems like it's an unfinished room with a halfway-built fireplace. There are more piles of lumber, stone, and even some old rusted masonry tools lying around the mantel and hearth. Bright tiles adorn the opening to the fireplace, each with colorful symbols, twelve in all.

"Hey, aren't those the same symbols we saw on the map?" Tinsley asks.

"Looks like it." I step closer. They look familiar, but without my phone, I can't compare them to the photo. "I don't know what they mean, but this has to be important." We don't have time to try to figure it out, but I'm definitely coming back to this once we get rid of the Sanderses.

I pick up an A-shaped tool with two pointy tips. "Check this out. It's just like the one on the lodge sign."

"Oh yeah!" Tinsley says. "And this looks pretty menacing." She holds up a long, rusted metal pole with a pointy end like a spear, which I think is an old fireplace poker.

Leo bends down and picks up a few U-shaped objects. "Horseshoes?" he says. "That's all that's left? Great."

"It's not like we're going to actually do anything, right?" I say. "We just have to look serious. We have to convince them we're able to fight them."

"It's like what you said about bears," Tinsley says. "We have to appear bigger than we are."

"Right." I pick up what looks like it used to be a wooden ax handle, and pass it to Leo. "Whatever we can find to make ourselves look and sound stronger and bigger, and hopefully it will scare them off."

"I hope this works," Leo says. He seems like he might be regretting his initial call to war.

"It will," I say. "You were right, the only way out of this is to fight back. We have to show them they can't mess with us anymore. Plus, the only way home is through them. We don't have a choice."

"Okay," he says, and takes a deep breath. "Let's defend the castle?"

We all laugh nervously. And then we head back through the rooms to the tower and out into the late-day sun, pushing through the wooden doors just as Aaron is about to enter. The dogs bound into the yard like nothing is happening, wagging their tails and barking.

All three of them jump back at first, startled by the dogs and our wild appearance and strange weapons. But they quickly realize who we are and regain their ground. "Get the heck out!" Aaron says. "What are you doing here?"

"We could ask you the same," I say.

"You're a disgusting mess," Michael says, laughing. Although he should talk. The three of them look like they've been in the woods for more than a week. "What's inside?"

"Not much, it's mostly empty," Leo says.

They don't wait for his answer, and they're not all that interested in us. Instead they go into the tower and pound up the steps to go explore.

We all look at one another. "What now?" Tinsley asks.

"Maybe they're too tired to fight," Leo says. "I mean, what have they been eating?"

"Good question." We probably should be taking this chance to leave, but all our things are still in the fireplace room, including my mom's camera. And maybe the Sanderses just don't have it in them anymore to want to fight us after three days of wandering on the mountain. We wait, listening to their voices echo through the castle as they do their own exploring.

Eventually we hear them heading back down the spiral stairs and talking about how cool the place is. "Dad is going to lose his mind over this place," Aaron says. "I can't believe he was right."

We look at one another. *Mr. Sanders knows they're here?*

They come back out. Very quickly we realize we should have taken the chance to run, and not given them the benefit of the doubt. Aaron walks right up to me, his face nearly in mine.

"You don't think you're getting credit for this, do you?" Aaron asks. "You"—he presses his finger into my shoulder—"aren't even from here. You think you and your famous little YouTube family can just move in and steal our town's biggest secret?"

Guess they finally figured out who I am. "I'm not stealing a secret," I say. "We found the directions, and we came to find it and did. End of story."

"Not happening," he says. "No one will believe you, anyway."

"It was her idea to come find it," Tinsley says. "She gets the credit. We're all witnesses. And we have it on video."

"Oh really?" Michael grabs Tinsley by the elbow and yanks her back away from us. "On this?" He holds up my mom's camera.

"Let me have that," I say.

Michael grins and shakes his head. "Come get it."

I clench my teeth. *Think, Lin, think.*

"Give it back to her!" Tinsley says. "It's not yours."

"Who made you boss?" Aaron says.

"Leave her alone," Leo says.

"Or what?"

Leo doesn't say anything.

"You're just like your brother—you talk too much." Now, Aaron shakes Tinsley's arm.

Seth steps up and sort of taps Aaron's arm. "Leave her be, man. Not worth it."

"Dude, we're in the middle of nowhere," Michael says. "We can do whatever we want." But Aaron lets go of Tinsley, and she quickly moves back over by us. Michael straps the camera over his chest. And that jerk is going to steal my mom's camera and all the work I've done.

"So this is what you three have been doing up here?" Aaron asks. "Looking for a legend? You think you get to claim it now, or something, like finders keepers?"

"No one can claim this," I say. "Not the way you're thinking anyway."

"Everything can be bought," Aaron says. "Our dad will turn this into a hotel. He's going to love this." He motions over the courtyard and gardens. "Take all this out, put in a giant swimming pool. Parking over there."

My stomach drops. We might have found this amazing place, only to have it turned into a vacation spot by Sanders Construction. My discovery could be claimed by this awful family. Annie Smith Peck would stake a claim and not let anyone else steal it. When you want something, you've got to go for it. No matter how impossible it seems.

I take a step forward, holding my walking stick like a staff and the pointed A-shaped tool as if it's a sword. "Why can't you just let it be? Why are you even here anyway? Just go home and leave us and the castle alone!"

"Ooooo!" Aaron and Michael howl at my challenge. They seem energized, not intimidated. Michael even takes pictures of us, with my camera, which infuriates me even more.

"She gets feisty!" Aaron says through his laughter.

"I'm serious." I step closer, ignoring Leo's and Tinsley's whispered warnings. "WE found this castle. It's up to us to decide what should happen to it."

They just laugh at me. Taunt us. Make faces and pretend to jump toward us in an attack. And I know we can't *actually* fight them. I realize there's a different challenge I need to present. One I can win.

I step back and whisper to Leo to call the dogs and get ready. They trot over happily, tongues lolling, tails wagging, no idea in the world that anything is amiss. "Stay," Leo tells them. They sit right next to him, despite the boys trying to coax them over.

"Leave. Them. Alone," Leo says, taking a step forward.

"Or. What. Hobbit boy." Aaron goes right up to Leo and this time grabs his shoulders hard. I think he's going to give Leo a big shake, but before he gets the chance, both dogs growl and jump on Aaron, pushing him down to the ground, hard on his butt.

"Get your mutts off me!" he screams. Leo calls them off,

and they listen immediately. I don't think they even bared their teeth, just jumped on him to protect Leo.

Aaron starts shouting something about his father suing Leo's family for a dog attack, but I cut him off.

"Listen! I have a proposal," I say.

They laugh more. But I know exactly how to put an end to this.

"It's a race. Simple as that. First person home gets to claim the discovery of the Castle in the Clouds. You have the proof in your hands." I point to the camera. It makes me feel sick thinking they have it, but if they think it's important, they won't ruin it. And we are on it so much, no one is going to think it's actually the Sanderses' footage. But they don't know that.

Aaron stops moving around and shuts his mouth. Michael looks at him, waiting for instructions, and Seth rolls his eyes. "You mean a literal race?" Aaron asks. "We'll all just run for it?"

"Yeah, why not? It's fair, right?" I say. "I mean, we know the way back. Don't you?"

Aaron looks at Michael, who shrugs. "All right. Deal," Aaron says. "There's no way you twerps will beat all three of us."

"Okay, then, game on," I say.

"Like right now?" Leo asks quietly behind me. "We're just going to run?"

"Yep," I say. And once more, I yell, "RUN."

But *this time*, I hold my arms out to block my friends, and we all stand still.

And the three boys take off through the tunnel and back into the woods alone.

20

"That was freaking genius!" Tinsley shouts once we know the boys are long gone. "Lin, you're a genius."

"I figured they'd be stupid enough to fall for it," I say. "It was better than trying to fight them."

"Yeah, that was going to end badly," Leo says. "Smart thinking. Now let's get out of here."

"But what about your mom's camera? Your documentary?" Tinsley asks.

I look out at the castle grounds, overgrown, crumbly, but magical. "I'm just going to take my chances, I guess. It's the only way I could see them leaving us alone." Standing here with them, taking it all in, even though I'm tired and hungry, I'm really proud of us. We're victorious. The only thing that bothers me is what Aaron said in the castle and how it sounded like his dad knows all about this place already.

I look up at the sky. We're never making it back before dark. "Do you still want to do a quick search?" I ask, hoping they say yes.

They both look exhausted.

"I'm starving," Tinsley says, nearly whining. Which I completely understand. I am also starving. Acknowledging it makes the raw, gnawing feeling even worse.

"Don't you think people might be out looking for us by now?" Leo asks. He's right, and three nights gone is going to put our parents into a major panic, if they aren't there already.

"Probably," Tinsley says. "But I'm so tired. I can't go anymore today."

"I'm sure they are," I say. "Maybe it's better we stay put." I'm not really sure anymore what the right thing to do is. My brain is so foggy I can't even think straight. "We could build a fire, scrape out the remainder of the almond butter. There were blueberries growing near the wall."

"What about water?" Leo asks. "I think we're almost out. And I'm worried about these guys too." He bends down to scratch the dogs, who pant wildly now.

"I still have some." I limp my way back into the castle to find my bag. I bring it out and pour some of it into the lid for Merlin and Little John. We share the rest. It's not a lot, but I think we'll be fine until morning.

"I still have the magic water straw AJ gave me," Tinsley mentions. "Which is awesome, if we find a creek."

"We will tomorrow for sure, when we head back," I say. "For now let's find something to eat." Reluctantly Leo and Tinsley help gather blueberries. I also find a ton of dandelions and violets, which my parents would sometimes throw in salads. I don't know how Leo and Tinsley feel about eating weeds, but it's better than nothing. We get lucky and find some wild strawberries too, which don't have much flavor but are edible. "All together we can make our own berry and weed salad," I say, with as much enthusiasm as I possibly can, even though I'd much rather be eating pizza with extra cheese. Or anything else.

Both of them look at me like I've lost it.

"Pretend we're on one of those survivalist shows," I say.

"With everything you've filmed, we basically are," Tinsley says. Her face lights up. "Maybe you could actually get your movie on TV and we'd all be famous!" She stops herself as though just remembering Michael stole my camera. "Oh. Never mind."

"I'm going to get it back," I say.

"That's assuming we survive," Leo says.

"We will survive. I promise."

We nibble on our foraged finds. The blueberries are good, but that's about it. After a few minutes of trying different combos of leaves and berries, we give up and head back into the castle for one last look around before it gets dark.

Normally I wouldn't recommend splitting up, especially after Tinsley getting lost, but it's not like we are going to get lost inside the castle. "Stay near the outer edges of the rooms. If you find anything interesting, or need help, just shout," I say, and we all begin inspecting different rooms. As I make my way around, I test boards out before I step fully on them, still anxious about falling through again. But for the most part every room seems sturdy enough for walking. They are just dimly lit since there are very few windows. The place starts to feel more like a dungeon than a castle. Who would want to live with hardly any light coming in? Vampires? *Let's not go there, Lin—now you're sounding like Tinsley.*

With one hand on the wall and one hand holding a flashlight, I find my way back to the room with the tiled fireplace to take a better look at the symbols. I know they're the same ones from the lodge, but without a way to interpret them, all I can think is there's simply something special about this fireplace.

It's huge, big enough for me to stand in, which I do, and shine the light up the chimney. The light disappears into the darkness. I try to brace myself with a foot on one side and a hand on the other to lift myself up and shine the light farther, in case something is hidden in the chimney, but suddenly the stone under my foot gives way. There's a loud scratching sound like something scraping across a chalkboard, just like when the slab of rock moved to reveal the doorway through the sheer side of the cliff.

I fall on my butt.

But the weird part is I'm also moving.

Or rather the floor under my butt is moving, and I'm going with it. The whole bottom and back wall of the fireplace turns, almost like I'm on a slow merry-go-round. The next thing I know, I'm in a brand-new room.

My jaw drops. This one is finished. And furnished. Gold and green velvet furniture and a long dining table with tall chairs. Massive plush sofas and oil paintings on the walls and candelabras on every surface. It feels like I've just stepped back in time.

There's even a candle flickering on a small table in the corner.

Which, all things considered, is a little weird.

Even weirder: In the shadows, I can see there's a person in a chair next to the table.

AJ.

"I was wondering whether or not you would show up," she says, crossing her legs.

"How? I mean, when did—?" I stumble over my words, trying to figure out what to even ask her first. How she got there or how she decorated so fast. "What the heck is going on?"

"Seeing as you're the trespassing party, I feel like I should be asking you that question." AJ stands up, walks over to the dining table where a cheese-and-cracker platter sits. She offers it to me, and I happily take some as I start to explain that I had no idea the fireplace could turn, but she waves her hand for me to stop. "I'm just teasing," she says. "I don't mind. I'm sure you have a lot of questions." She glances down at my ripped pants and bandaged legs. "What happened to you?"

"Let's just say not all the rooms in this place are as nice as this," I say between mouthfuls of buttery crackers. "I need to get Leo and Tinsley. Do you live here?"

"Sometimes," she says. "This place belonged to my seven-times great-aunt."

"Aunt?"

AJ nods. "I'm actually named for her: Anna Pace."

It suddenly occurs to me that her initials, which were on the sword on the tapestry at the lodge, are the same as Arthur Pendragon's—*AP*. "People have been looking for this forever and you've been here the whole time?"

"Not the *whole* time. I only finally found it a few years ago. Been adding things slowly over time."

"And no one knows you're here?"

AJ shakes her head. "I don't think so. Pretty sure I'm the only person who knew it truly existed. Well . . . now I'm not." She doesn't seem upset about it, though. "Does it bother you that you didn't get here first?" She gives me a friendly smirk.

"No," I say, surprising myself because it had seemed important at one time to get here first, but now I feel like I'm part of the story. "Actually, I'm even more interested to know more." I need to go get my friends, but I really want to hear what AJ knows first.

"Well, I can tell you my aunt was the only female stone-mason of her time. Pretty scandalous, actually. She was a teen-ager when she started, and had apprenticed with her father. But she frequently dressed as a man in order to do some of the church and cathedral jobs; otherwise they wouldn't have hired her. She designed and built this place based on a much bigger castle from Scotland. She brought a crew with her, of course, and had hopes of living out the rest of her years here. At least that's what the family has always thought."

"What happened?"

"She died young, before it was done. The crew sealed it off, honoring her wishes that no one else should have it. She never married, didn't have any kids. At the time she thought she was the last of the Paces. Little did she know her parents would have one more child after she left Scotland. But they'd never had any contact with her, so she had no idea she had a little brother. That younger brother's family would grow, and generations later—Enter: me—stumble into a family legacy."

"That's incredible. How did you get in, though? When we reached the rock wall door, it was buried. Had been buried for years."

"That must be the east entrance. There are several tunnels in."

I sit down on a plush green sofa. "And all along we thought this was somehow connected to King Arthur."

AJ smiles. "Like Arthur of the knights' table and Excalibur and all?"

I nod sheepishly. "It's not, though, is it?"

AJ shrugs. "You know what they say about legends, don't you?"

"No?"

"They have to start somewhere."

"So, you're saying your aunt *is* connected to King Arthur."

AJ takes a sip of her drink and says nothing.

"Are you related to him? You have the same initials as he does—*AP*."

Still nothing.

I try a different tactic, asking another question on my mind. "We saw you in the hardware store. Making a key. Was that for the Freemason lodge?"

AJ smiles. "You're clever. Yes, I was making myself a copy." She gets up and opens one of the drawers of a big cabinet and pulls out a ring of keys. She tosses them to me. "I meant to return these, but at the time didn't know who they belonged to." Then she leans forward with a very serious look on her face. "The Freemasons are a cool bunch, but I got tired of them keeping everything behind closed doors, keeping the truth of this place in the dark."

"What truth?"

"That women have built castles. I just have to find the proof so they can't dispute it."

I lean against the table and pop a grape in my mouth. It bursts with a glorious sweetness, like the best thing I've ever tasted. I'm starting to worry about being separated from Leo and Tinsley for so long. They are probably wondering where I am, and they could use some of this food, but I can't stop myself from asking, "What proof?"

AJ purses her lips together in thought. "This is quite the

interrogation." She sits and leans forward in her chair, elbows on knees, and says, "They have always been very interested about this place, but they never found it. I don't think there were a lot of serious attempts, to be honest, but they still knew a lot and I suspect they have documents of my aunt's immigration, possibly even early drafts of her designs in that lodge under lock and key, but I have not yet found them."

"Seems like a silly thing to be so protective about. Why not share it with the world?" I ask.

AJ pauses and then says, "There was, let's say, some confusion, when she came over and they claimed that she stole a very valuable artifact from Freemasons in Scotland. Whatever she *stole* is what they are actually protecting."

My heart beats a little faster. I get up and start pacing the room. "An artifact?" This is far more exciting than I could have ever imagined, and AJ has chosen *me* to share her family story. Figures I don't have my camera! "Like what, like a crown or a chalice or something?"

"I'm not sure. That's why I was hoping to find those documents. Sometimes they list what belongings people had with them on the boat."

"So you've been living in this castle and searching for those papers?"

"Well, I can't spend my whole life here. I take seasonal jobs and travel in between. But on and off, yes." AJ nods. "Not with any real consistency and definitely no luck."

"This is the coolest thing I've ever heard!" I want so many

more details, but I have to get my friends in here. "Can you wait one sec? I have to get Leo and Tinsley."

"Take some of that with you." She gestures toward the cheese-and-cracker platter and hands me a pitcher of water. I gather as much as I can in my shirt and walk back into the fireplace. AJ follows me. She presses a giant stone, and suddenly, before I get a chance to ask her to wait for us, I'm turning around again, back into the original room.

"Leo! Tinsley!" I shout from the doorway. "Come here quick!"

I wait a minute and then hear footsteps. "Where are you?" Leo calls from the hall.

"In the room where we got the tools!"

Leo pops his head in, Tinsley right behind him with Merlin and Little John. "You've been in here the whole time?" Tinsley asks. "I swear I checked this room," she says to Leo.

"You're *not* going to believe what just happened." I hold out my shirt for them to see the cheese and crackers, and they both gasp. And then I hand Tinsley the ring of keys.

"No way!" she says, and then tucks them in her pocket. "How—" she starts to ask, but shoves cheese in her mouth instead.

"Where did you get this?" Leo asks as he helps himself to a handful of grapes.

"Behind the fireplace," I say. "AJ *lives* here. Sort of."

"*Behind* the fireplace?" Tinsley asks with a mouthful of cheese. "What does that mean?"

"It's a secret room! I think maybe that's why the fireplace has those symbols—the ones that match the tapestry at the lodge, which had to belong to the original Anna Pace!" Both of their faces are blank.

"The original who?" Leo asks.

I realize I have a lot to explain. "Just wait. You have to see it. It's amazing. She said she's looking for proof about who built this, and there is something hidden somewhere, just like you said, Tinsley. Some artifact, AJ thinks, that would prove her ancestor was here. AJ just doesn't know what that artifact could be."

Leo walks over to it, inspecting the stones and tiles. "I don't see anything."

I try pushing different parts of the chimney and wall, but nothing happens. "My foot pressed one of these stones, and it just turned. Suddenly I was in a fully furnished room, with AJ. I swear!"

"Obviously you were somewhere, because you came back with a feast," Tinsley says.

I slap my hand on the stones as hard as I can. "AJ? Can you hear me? Let us in! Please. Maybe we can help!"

Nothing but silence. It's as if it never happened. Even though we're eating the proof. I don't understand why she won't let us back in. We keep trying to move different stones, but nothing happens until suddenly Leo accidently knocks one of the cornerstones off the fireplace. It hits the floor with a loud *thunk*.

"There's something behind this one," he says, pulling at a piece of dusty burlap. It rips away, and more stones fall to the floor. I cringe as we totally destroy the fireplace. Leo reveals more, and beneath is a dull but smooth metal blade. "That looks like a sword," he whispers, his eyes wide and excited.

"Get it!" Tinsley shouts. He pulls the burlap down farther, which rips away plaster and dust. More stones plunk to the floor. The last bit he pulls away reveals something white and thin, like pale-colored sticks.

Or bones. Five of them. Fingers.

"Um, guys," Tinsley whispers. "Is that what I think it is?"

Leo stumbles back first. "Ohmygodthatsa . . . hand!" He trips over a pile of lumber and falls on his butt, and then quickly scrambles to his feet.

I don't say anything. Definitely never stumbled on a body before. No awesome advice from Mom ringing in my head. Only a slight twist in my gut, probably from eating too much cheese.

We all stare at the hand bones for a very long time. I'm not sure why AJ doesn't open the secret fireplace door again. Maybe she can't hear us through the thick stone walls. But she knows we're out here, so why wouldn't she come looking? Plus, she *needs* this sword. It has to be the artifact she was looking for.

"So who's going to do it?" I finally ask.

"Do what?" Tinsley whispers. "Don't say what I think you're going to say."

"We have to get that sword."

Tinsley shakes her head. "I knew you were going to say that."

"Don't you agree?" I look at both of them, and then I give them the short version of everything AJ told me. "I'd much rather see AJ get to claim this castle for her family than Mr. Sanders turning it into a hotel. This has to be what she needs. We pull it out, and if she doesn't come out of there, we'll bring it home and keep it safe. She knows how to find us."

Leo takes a deep breath and nods. "I agree. Let's do it all together."

Tinsley cringes, but she joins us. We all put one hand on the hilt, and I count to three.

"One, two, three!"

We pull the sword out as hard as we can, and a little more dust and crumbly stone comes with it. It's heavy and the blade end clangs to the floor, but we manage not to drop it. Gently we lay the whole thing on the floor, and I dust it off with my shirt.

There are two curly initials on the hilt. *AP*.

"Arthur Pendragon?" Leo asks with so much awe in his voice, I feel bad having to tell him otherwise.

"Anna Pace," I say. "AJ's great-something-aunt. She must have carved her initials on it after she stole it."

"That tapestry at the lodge," Tinsley says. "Like you said, Lin. The symbols are on the fireplace, and the initials are on the sword. How cool! I can't wait to tell my dad."

I'm not sure if AJ would want us to tell the Freemasons

about all of this. Kind of feels like it should be her call. But I don't say anything to Tinsley right now. We can figure that out later. The bigger problem at hand is getting home in the first place.

"You don't still want to sleep in the castle, do you?" Leo asks. "With that?" He points to the bones in the fireplace. He shakes his head as if to convince me I do not. "We don't even know who that hand belongs to," he whispers.

"We'll sleep in a different room," I say, and then turn back to the fireplace. I bang on the inside of it as hard as I can with a piece of broken stone. We all call out AJ's name, and after a minute or two, the fireplace makes that awful scratching sound again. "Hurry," I say, pulling each of them closer to me. "Squeeze in together!"

"What about the dogs?" Leo says. "I can't leave them!"

"We'll have AJ help us come back for them and the sword," I say. "Don't worry, Leo, we won't leave them."

Leo looks a little uncertain but calls out, "I'll be right back, boys! Stay!" The dogs sit and wag their tails and seem completely unbothered by the fact that the fireplace is swallowing us up.

On the other side, AJ greets us with a large metal pole that looks a bit like a harpoon. "Ah, the whole crew!" she says. "Welcome!"

"You're not going to believe what we found," I say. "You have to come to the other side with me. The dogs are still there too."

"No problem," she says. "I'm intrigued! Let's make it a little easier on ourselves and use the door." AJ winks and uses the pole to pull down on a rope that hangs to the side of the fireplace. Suddenly a paneled wall with floor-to-ceiling bookshelves opens up to the left of the fireplace, which then opens to the room next to the fireplace room. She leads us around to where Merlin and Little John are still waiting. And then she sees the mess. She looks at me.

"Sorry. It was an accident. But look!" I go over to the sword and attempt to lift it. I get it about halfway up, and she joins me to raise it upright. She covers her mouth with her other hand and looks between the three of us, sort of shaking her head in disbelief.

"Is that what you were looking for?" Tinsley asks.

"I think so, Pinkie." AJ rubs her thumb over the dull blade, shining it a tiny bit. "I had no idea it would be something so spectacular. It was in the wall of the fireplace?"

Leo, who's crouched by the dogs and cleaning his glasses, says, "Yep, and that's not the only thing we found." He points up to the gaping hole in the crumbling stone. "Any idea who left that behind?" he asks.

AJ goes over to study the hand. She looks real close but doesn't touch it. "I have no idea. But wow. You three made quite the discovery. Let's bring this back with us," she says, pointing to the sword, "but we'll leave that for now. You two look hungry."

"You have no idea," Tinsley says. We follow AJ back into

her secret room, and she shuts the bookcases behind us. She lays the dusty sword across the table and then gets out more snacks for Tinsley and Leo and the dogs. Cheese and strawberries and water with real ice cubes. Leo and I sit on the couch, AJ on her overstuffed chair, and Tinsley sits on a giant cushioned windowsill big enough to be a bed.

"How do you have all this food?" I ask. "There's no electricity."

"Small generator," AJ says. "I crank it, and it's enough to keep the little fridge going. I use candles at night. But no phones or chargers, so don't bother asking about that. I'm not usually here very long, though. Anyway, enough about me," she says as she pulls her legs up under her on the chair. "I want to know your story. How did you three get this far? How did you find me?"

All three of us start talking at once—Leo and Tinsley explaining how they grew up hearing about the legend and me about who my family is and how I got involved—and then we all start cracking up. "Go ahead, Tinsley," I say. "You start."

Tinsley looks surprised for a minute, but then launches into everything she's ever heard from her dad and his friends. She tells AJ about the photo, her family's interest in the castle, and about her dad being bedridden right now.

Leo tells her about the Sanderses, how they followed us up and they know about the castle too, and how their father has a habit of gobbling up every property in town.

"Leo also knows everything there is to know about King Arthur," I say. "Which is how we put things all together."

Leo's face turns red. "Yeah, but Lin, you figured out the symbols were simply landmarks."

"I wouldn't have if you didn't suggest they were like a map key."

"And I wouldn't be here at all if it weren't for you two," Tinsley says.

AJ has a funny look on her face. "Well, aren't you three adorable. So, how are you getting home? I'm assuming by now the national guard is probably out looking for you."

Her joke brings me back to reality like a punch in the gut. "Yeah, we need to get home as quickly as possible. Our parents are going to be—"

The three of us look at one another, but none of us finish the sentence. Leo drops his gaze to the dogs. Tinsley glances out the window. I think the realization is too much to even say out loud. The worry we've caused alone is going to be hard to face. This is part of the adventure that I didn't want to feel, a dreadful weight looming more than ever. I drop the strawberry I was about to eat on the plate.

"First thing tomorrow," AJ says as she gets up and pulls a few blankets out of a giant trunk. "We will all head out together. For now, have your fill, please. You can get a good night's sleep, and you'll all feel better in the morning." She hands me a first-aid kit. "You can clean up your legs a little bit with that."

"Thanks," I say, and take the kit.

She hands us each a blanket and then starts lighting extra

candles. We're quiet as we watch the room brighten. The light flickers on the stone walls and casts shadows all around. Tinsley sits with her back up against the frame of the window. Leo sits on the floor with the dogs on either side of him, but he gets up to help me unwrap the cuts on my legs to clean and rewrap. AJ finds a cloth and begins polishing the sword.

"Where did those symbols come from anyway?" I ask her. "Did your aunt do that?"

AJ shakes her head. "I actually don't know. Possibly? I'm not sure why she would, though. More likely it's someone who found the castle long before I came along."

"The person behind the fireplace," Leo suggests in a whisper as he looks up at me. I shiver at the thought. But maybe Leo is right. I dab at the worst gash with an antiseptic, and it stings like crazy. Once it's dry I apply a new Band-Aid and it feels so much better.

"Maybe it was a Freemason from long ago who came looking," I say. "He could have marked the trail so he could come back, or lead others. Only he never returned."

AJ gets a playful smirk on her face. "Are you suggesting my aunt was a murderer?"

"Oh no!" I say, but now that she mentions it, that's exactly what I was unknowingly coming to conclusion with. "But who else would have been here to do it?"

"Geesh," Tinsley says. "Talk about family drama."

AJ stands up the sword so we can see her work. "We'll get to the bottom of it. For now, check out this beauty."

Leo gets up and goes over to see up close. "Wow," he says. "This is so amazing. I've never seen anything like it. How do you think your aunt got it here?"

"Good question," AJ says. "A big box, maybe a trunk. Want to give it a try?" she asks him.

"Can I?"

AJ lifts it down to the floor and stands it in front of Leo, who isn't much taller than it. "You might need to grow into it a bit," she says, laughing. Leo lifts it off the ground a few inches, but that's about it. It's a massive sword; I can't imagine even my dad wielding it. The hilt is decorated with intricate designs surrounding the initials *AP*.

"It's funny the Freemasons had all these clues and connections to King Arthur when really it was your aunt all along," I say.

"I think she probably enjoyed the connection herself," AJ says. "It was a good way to disguise herself, and she'd been doing that her whole life anyway. She probably just let them run with it." AJ lays the sword back on the table and carefully wraps it up in a large sheet.

We talk a little longer about what she'll do with the sword and how she plans on getting it back to Scotland. Before we know it, we're all cozy and starting to yawn from the long day when the supermoon rises and shines through Tinsley's window like a great luminescent planet. The view is otherworldly, and we all go over to get a better look. It's so bright it lights up the woods and deep valley below. The river is a silvery thin snake way below, and the moon seems close enough to reach out and touch. My dad would be speechless. It reminds me of the storybook my parents would read me when I was little, one I'd forgotten about until now, the refrain suddenly fresh in my mind: *I love you to the moon and back*. All three of us in different places tonight, but at least we're all sharing the same moon.

I fall asleep that night on AJ's couch, Leo and I feet to feet, warm and full, and happy to be hiking home tomorrow.

22

In the morning, I wake up before my two friends. AJ is feeding the dogs treats in between packing a bag and creating some kind of interesting leather strap to carry the sword on her back. She looks like someone out of a fantasy story, sort of medieval and magical all at once. I stretch and yawn, and there's a tiny flicker of a dream I had of my mother in the back of my mind.

She'd been crouching along a riverbed, scooping sparkling water by the handfuls, and beckoned me to come drink. *Remember everything I taught you*, she said without moving her mouth. *The way is inside you.*

It's all I can remember. And I have no idea what she means by *the way*. But picturing her now, lit up by the sun and smiling at me, makes me even more eager to get home. I wake up Leo and Tinsley.

Tinsley sits up from her window bed, rubs her eyes, and looks at Leo and me like she forgot where she was.

"I was dreaming I was in my tree house," she says. "But I'm not."

"No, but you will be by tonight," I say.

AJ offers us some bread, orange juice, and leftover fruit before we gather up our bags and leave the castle behind. The dogs trot ahead of us, happy and carefree, but walking across the courtyard is bittersweet for the three of us, I think. I wish I had my camera for some parting footage, which makes me angry at those boys all over again. Regardless, I'm happy to be heading home so that everyone knows we are okay.

"AJ?" I ask. "Do you think we could come back again sometime?"

"I don't see why not," she says. "Now that I have the sword, and I can try to get it to its proper owners, I think the castle would be best enjoyed by everyone."

"You don't want to live in it?" Tinsley asks. "I'd want to live in it forever."

"I'm ready to move on now," AJ says. "Let's head this way. I know a different way down."

She leads us to a different corner of the courtyard than where we came in from. There's an old iron gate so covered with branches and vines you can't even see it until she removes several of them. We help her uncover the gate the rest of the way, and on the other side, the bushes are so dense we have to squeeze through single file. After we're through, looking back it just seems like a hedgerow of sorts. You can't see the gate at all.

"I've taken a few different paths up here, but I think this will be the shortest way back to town," she says.

I'm a little hesitant to say anything, but since I woke up I've had this thought we would go straight down the west side of the cliff to the river. Even though west doesn't seem quite right based on how we got up here, I can't get it out of my head. I don't know if it was my dream or just remembering that the river flows toward town or what. And AJ knows these woods probably better than anyone, definitely better than I do. She'd know the fastest way. So I don't say anything as we plunge into the woods.

"What do you think will happen to the castle, then?" Tinsley asks.

"If the Freemasons do have those documents that tie everything together—my aunt, the sword, the building plans—we'll all be on the same page. I don't know what will be involved, but maybe somehow it can be opened to the public."

"Someone with a lot of money could preserve it," Leo says. "Or turn it into a private resort." Merlin and Little John trot next to him, looking up at his face every so often, almost like they are asking when we will be back home.

"We'll have to see what happens," AJ says. For nearly an hour, she continues to lead us over rocky ridges and through dense underbrush. I feel more and more uneasy about the direction we're going. Not because I think AJ has any ulterior motives, but because I think she's taking us the wrong way, or at least not the best way. It seems to me if we keep heading in this direction, we'll end up taking more time up on the ridge than necessary. That was the route we came up because of Mr. Holiday's directions to the symbols, but if we're just trying to get home fast, straight down to the river and following it to town is the better choice. The longer I don't say anything and the more steps we make, the more my stomach twists in knots. I just keep picturing my father and Leo's mom trudging through the woods and calling our names. Poor Tinsley's mom probably not able to leave her dad's side to help look. But I don't want to go against AJ—she has to know what she's doing. And I've made enough mistakes as it is.

And then suddenly I remember the trail map Dad had pulled out when he first started talking about going on a moonlit hike. There was a service road that wraps around the base of the mountain and follows the trail for quite a distance. Not much of a road, more like a grassy path wide enough for trucks and used for forestry maintenance or emergencies. If anyone was out looking for us, that's exactly where they'd be parked.

"Wait!" I shout. "I just remembered something."

Everyone stops for a minute and looks at me, including the dogs, who I startled.

"There's a service road. If we head toward that it'll take us straight to town. It'll be so much faster."

Tinsley and Leo look at AJ.

AJ seems to consider my idea, but says, "I don't remember seeing it in my treks up here. Are you sure?"

"I'm a thousand times positive," I say. "My dad had a map out on the counter before we left. I remember seeing it. If we head down and east, we should run right into it."

AJ looks at the sky, and her compass, and then she gives me a strong nod. "Lead the way."

My heart feels like it beats harder than it's supposed to. I know I'm right, but there's still a little bit of fear that if I'm wrong I'll get us more lost. But AJ probably wouldn't go along with it if she thought it was too risky. We start making the arduous trek down, nearly straight down, which is much harder than following the ridge.

After several stumbles and slides, Leo stops and finds walking sticks for all of us.

"Thanks," I say.

"I learned from the best," he says. And we keep heading down. It's hard on our knees, and there are areas that have small rock cliffs that we have to drop ourselves down from. None of it is impossible, however, and even Merlin and Little John hang on. Bit by bit, we edge ourselves east, moving in a diagonal way down the hillside. After about two hours of this, we're exhausted. It takes more strength going down such a steep hill, to keep yourself balanced, to not tumble head over heels all the way down. Looking at the decline, that would be bad.

But soon the hill starts to level out, and then just ahead of me, I see a grassy cleared-out area. "That has to be it!" I point them to the clearing. We all step onto the road and it's the biggest relief I've had in days. I think about my mom in my dream: She said the way was inside me. She was right. Now all we have to do is follow the way out.

"Nice work!" Leo says.

"I'm impressed," AJ says. "Shouldn't be too far from here."

"I kind of want to run," Tinsley says. She jumps up and down a little bit.

"Save your energy, Pinkie," AJ says, shaking her head. "Slow and steady wins the race."

Grinning, I pick up my pace a little bit. I can be steady, but I don't know about slow. We're almost home, and I can't wait to see my dad so he knows I'm safe. It's only a few minutes of walking before we hear voices. Up ahead of us coming up the road we see Mr. Holiday. He pauses for a minute like he's not sure what he's seeing.

"Hey!" he shouts. "They're here!"

And then Jackson from the library appears, and Nelson from Dad's house crew, a police officer, and more people from town I don't know, and then Leo's mom, and then finally, my dad. I run right toward him. His usual cheeky smile and enthusiastic eyes have been replaced by exhaustion and fear. Everyone rushes around us at once. One of the men radios someone else on a walkie-talkie. "We've got them! They're safe!"

My dad wraps his arms around me, and we both cry. I

apologize a dozen times. Dad just holds me tight and says, over and over, "You're safe, kiddo. You're safe. That's all that matters to me."

Within a matter of seconds, more people come out from all directions and start attending to all of us. An entire search party of Newbridge residents. Someone wraps our necks with cool towels and gives us water bottles.

"Simon!" Tinsley shouts as an older boy emerges from the trees. He runs over to her and gives her a huge hug just as a park ranger on a four-wheeler pulls up. Then there's a second and a third and the whole thing is so overwhelming. There must be twenty-five or more people around us.

"All these people were out looking for us?" I whisper to my dad, feeling terrible.

We should have turned around earlier; we never should have kept going. I'd just wanted to prove myself, but I could have hurt my friends in the process. Thank goodness that didn't happen, but looking at this crowd it's obvious people still got hurt. Leo's mom glares at me, and she whisks him and the dogs away to one of the rangers. I don't get a chance to say anything before they drive off.

"Are you mad?" I ask, looking at my dad's haggard face.

"Not yet," Dad says. "Ask me again tomorrow when the shock of losing you and then finding you four days later wears off."

"Does Mom know?"

"Of course she knows. She was supposed to fly home yesterday but couldn't get a flight quick enough. Probably arriving at the airport pretty soon, actually." He checks his phone. "No service. We'll call her as soon as we're out of the woods."

I drop my head in my hands. Even though it's what I wanted, to make Mom come home, this was not *how* I wanted it. "She didn't have to do that. I wanted her to see what I could do and I wanted her to want to come home, but not like this."

"Lin, honey, she wants nothing more than to come home and see you safe. She's your mother. Do you really think she'd just sit back and let me deal with our lost daughter all by myself?"

"I just mean, I'm fine. She's coming home for nothing now."

"She loves you. No matter where she's at, you are her priority." Dad squeezes me. "I think that's exactly what she's *hoping*, that she's coming home for nothing. What were you three *thinking*, anyway? Thank goodness Mr. Holiday told us that you'd been in the shop asking all kinds of questions about the castle; otherwise we'd have had no idea where to look."

Before I'm able to tell him everything that's happened, a booming voice comes out of the crowd.

"Anyone see my boys?" A large man with clothes too fancy for the woods, and freshly combed and styled hair, stands with his hands on his hips. I can smell the sharp spice of his cologne from here. He waves a cell phone up in the air, trying to catch a signal. No one has an answer for him, and a couple apologize. He looks around, his eyes settle on me and Tinsley, and then he asks again. "Aaron and Michael. Weren't they with *you*?"

Then it sinks in. Just as we all joked.

The Sanders brothers never made it home.

23

The search party, which was led by Mr. Holiday because he knew part of the way up, stays to keep looking for the Sanderses and Seth, but more rangers on four-wheelers arrive to bring us all home. Simon takes Tinsley back. AJ seemingly disappears, but I imagine she ducked out of the swarming crowd to avoid attention. I wish she'd told us where she was going and what was next for the sword, but we're off the mountain in minutes and I'm so relieved it's all over. Not the adventure part, but the secrets and lies and worry I've caused.

At the trailhead, more people from town, and even some reporters, are standing around their parked cars and trucks on the side of the road, and they greet and welcome us home. If we hadn't been "missing" for so long, it might feel like we're heroes returning home from a voyage, but instead I feel pretty guilty. My dad rushed me right past everyone, even the reporters shouting questions at us. It seems all of Newbridge came together to look for us, and that makes me feel a little like winning a game by cheating.

Once we're back at the bus, my dad says, "Shower first. I'll call Mom and make you some eggs, okay? And then we're talking."

The hot water feels like heaven, and I stay in the shower for as long as our small water tank will allow. It's plenty, though. I feel like I haven't been clean in a year. Dirt and leaves and dried blood from my legs swirl down the drain. I can't believe what a mess I was, but there's something about it that actually makes me smile. *We did it*. We had a successful expedition. Not without injury, or obstacle, but we proved the castle was real, learned the true story behind it, and even found a sword to help AJ prove it. Which is good, considering my camera is probably long gone. *Mom's* camera. The thought makes me guilty all over again.

When I dry off I change into a long T-shirt and shorts. Out in the main area of the bus Dad is waiting with gauze and ointment to treat my cuts properly. And I finally get the chance to tell him everything. Everything from how sad I was about Mom leaving me, to Leo first mentioning the castle, to the Sanderses following us, and all that we ran into while we were up there. I even tell him about the bathroom stall at camp, and how humiliated and angry it made me that I didn't know what to do in that situation.

As he wraps the final cut with tape, he says, "Wow. That is quite the story."

"It's all true. Even the bones in the fireplace. I swear."

"I believe you. And I'm sorry camp was so awful. I wish

you'd told me right from the beginning." He gently squeezes my foot. "We maybe could have avoided a lot of fear and man-power."

I rest my head on his shoulder. "I'm really, really sorry, Dad."

"I can't wait to see the castle. Truly." He pats my knee. "Now, how do your legs feel?"

"Much better. Thanks, Dad." I'm not sure when is the best time to tell him Michael Sanders actually stole the video camera, but I'm thinking it's not right now. They still have to find those boys, and as much as I don't like them, I am a little worried for them, camera or no camera.

He checks his watch. "Mom should be here within the hour. I'd like for you to go lie down for a little while. Rest and think about things a little bit. We're going to have a family discussion about what happens from here on out, okay?"

"Okay." I can tell by his voice he means what consequences I'll be suffering from this and for how long. I'm guessing until I'm twenty.

"The most important thing for you is water and sleep."

"Okay." Truthfully, nothing sounds better.

He hugs me and hands me a glass of water. I retreat to my loft bed, shut the curtain, and stare out the skylight window. I am tired, but I'm also worried about Leo and Tinsley and what kind of trouble they might be getting in. I'm excited to see my mom, but also dreading facing the fact of why she's coming home. And the events of the past few days are all spinning in my head, dying to be written down or made into a movie, just like I imagined.

I'm even thinking about the boys still up in the woods somewhere. At least that part wasn't my fault—at least I don't think it was. I'm sure the search party will find them . . . I mean, how far could they have gotten? Maybe it was wrong of me to trick them the way I did. Maybe I should have worked harder at making us all get along and come home together. I tried to do all the right things. I fall into a deep, dreamless sleep until I suddenly wake up to my parents' voices.

They're talking in the kitchen, so I jump out of bed. My head throbs a bit, but I run in and see the most beautiful woman sitting there. She opens her arms wide.

"Mom!" I slide in on the bench next to her.

"Oh, baby girl!" She squeezes me so tight. "You terrified us. What were you *thinking*?"

"I was thinking it would only be one night and that by the time anyone knew we were gone, we'd be almost back home."

She holds me out to examine my face. She's tanned and freckled and her reddish-brown hair seems lighter than usual. "I'm so sorry," I say. "I never meant for it to go so long. Did Dad tell you everything?" I look at him, and he nods.

Mom gently holds my face in her hands, forcing me to look at her. "I know you didn't intend for it to go so long, but, Lin!

Everything I've taught you! You can't wander into the wilderness without being prepared."

"But I was, Mom! I promise. We had food and water for two days, which we made last almost double, plus we shared with the dogs." I explain to her all our preparations and supplies, basically the entire plan and the fact that we ran into AJ, twice, who gave us food. "It just went wrong because of the rain and those boys chasing us. Otherwise it never would have taken so long."

She smooths back my hair, and her shoulders relax a little bit. "Regardless, you shouldn't be roaming in the woods without a parent."

"You've always said we have to grab what we want. Dad says, 'Go find adventure.' That's exactly what I did!"

They look at each other for a second, but then Dad says, "You also broke into the Freemason lodge in town."

"How did you know that?" I ask, realizing my trouble just tripled.

"When you all went missing, the first thing the police did was look at security cameras in town to see what you've been up to the last week. To make sure you weren't kidnapped from a store or the park or wherever."

"Oh. We weren't kidnapped."

"And thank goodness for that," Mom says. "But trespassing? That's not something we can stand by, Lin. Can you explain yourself?"

No reason is going to be good enough for them, but I try to explain we didn't do any harm. "We were searching for clues. We didn't take anything from the lodge; we only looked around."

"It doesn't matter. You were breaking and entering," Mom says.

"No, we didn't! We had keys."

Mom gives me a look that says I better not press it, and I fall silent. I don't even know why I'm arguing except that I was hoping to talk about the exciting part of the past few days, not only all the things I did wrong. I tug at the strings of my cutoff shorts and wait for my sentencing.

"What's my punishment?" I ask.

My parents are quiet for an agonizing minute while I stare at the table until Mom says, "I don't know yet. We have to discuss it."

I can't stop the tears when I say, "Please, please, please, just don't send me back to camp." I rest my head on my arms, thinking for sure that's what they were planning.

Dad sighs. "We won't make you go back to camp. But there will be consequences for this. You're not going anywhere for a while."

The huge weight on my chest lifts away, and I rest my head on Mom's shoulder. "I was so afraid. I thought I could do it all right, Mom. I did remember so much of what you've taught me, it was like you were with me the whole time whispering in my head. But it was so hard to do. Things kept happening that I had no control over."

She rubs my back. "Yeah, that's part of backpacking. Or climbing or camping or traveling anywhere. You can't control weather and animals, and in your case, other people. It can be dangerous, even to someone who is very smart, don't get me wrong, but inexperienced. Do you understand?"

"I do, yes."

"And I'm pretty sure we won't see anything like this ever again?"

"No, Mom," I sniffle. "I promise. I'm so sorry I made you come home."

"You didn't *make* me come home, sweetheart. I *wanted* to come home and make sure you were okay."

"I just wanted to go with you," I whisper. "And then when I couldn't, I wanted to do something you wouldn't want to miss and you'd come home."

"Oh, honey," she sighs, and pulls me close. "*You* are my home. You're my greatest adventure. I'm so proud of you, and once I've calmed down from all of this, I can't wait to hear about all the amazing things that happened with you and your friends. I love sharing adventures with you. We might not be together all the time, but I love you no matter where we are."

She hugs me again, hands me a tissue, and then gets up to make us some tea. The rest of the night the three of us talk about the hike to the castle, the amazing footage I captured and lost, and how close Leo and Tinsley and I became.

"And AJ," I yawn over my tea. "Oh, you would love her, Mom. She's the coolest. She's just like Annie Peck Smith, and her family's story is so interesting, and . . ." I yawn again before I can finish my sentence.

"Let's save the rest of that for morning, okay?" Mom says, placing my cup in the sink and smiling at me so brightly I truly do feel like her greatest adventure.

24

Early the next morning, there's loud banging on our door. I'm still in bed and fuzzy headed from sleeping when I hear it. Everything is a little sore from the past few days—stiff calves and thighs, achy back and head. It's almost like I'm just getting over the flu. Other than that I feel pretty rested, but I still haven't heard from Leo or Tinsley, so I'm starting to worry they are in worse trouble than me. I send them each a quick text to check in. And then I hear the persistent, loud knocking again.

"Dad?"

Nothing. He must be in the Victorian. Probably showing Mom all the work he's done while she's been away. I throw the covers off and slide out of bed to the floor. Outside the bus stand two police officers and Mr. Sanders. My insides freeze. The only thing I can think is, even though they would have no idea, I'm in trouble for what I said that sent the boys running. And now missing.

"What can we do for you, Officers?" my dad suddenly says

from behind them. I take my hand off the doorknob and eavesdrop. They all turn and shake hands with my parents.

"Is everything okay?" Mom asks.

"No, Mrs. Moser, everything is not," Mr. Sanders says. "My boys are still out there."

One of the officers elaborates. "As well as Seth Dolan. The search party came up empty yesterday. They had to end the search by dark, and they are grouping together now for another go at it, but there was some indication that your daughter might have an idea of where the three of them are, or at least a better idea than we do."

"Lin is exhausted, sir," Mom says. "If she knew where they were, she would have said something yesterday."

"I'm sure you're right, ma'am," the officer says. "But would you mind if we asked her a few questions anyway?"

My parents look at each other. "I don't know if this is a great idea," my dad says. "We could speak to her when she wakes up and let you know?"

"Pardon my frankness," the officer says. "But the window of opportunity is quickly closing. It's been five days."

I can see the struggle on my parents' faces. They want to help, but also want to protect me.

Mr. Sanders steps forward and points a finger at my dad. "My boys shouldn't have to suffer because they were up on a mountain messing around with your kid. It was her idea to go up there in the first place."

"Now, wait one minute." My dad straightens up. I've never seen him look so serious. "As far as we know, your kids followed my kid, and then they got themselves lost. They weren't *messing around* together."

"All I know is my boys never set foot up in those hills and wouldn't do so unless they were enticed."

My mom lets out a snort. "Are you kidding me right now? Our daughter and her friends went on an overnight hike. They had supplies and knew what they were doing. Mostly. No one *enticed* anyone!"

Go, Mom! I can't help but smile. The officers try to interrupt the argument before it gets any more heated, and that's when I open the door.

"I can answer any questions you have," I say. All heads turn to me. "I don't know where they are, but I know where we last saw them, if that helps."

"Lin, you're up?" Dad says.

"You think I could sleep through all this?" I wave at all of them. "Let me get changed, and I'll be right out."

Everyone seems okay with this, so I go back to find clothes and grab my phone and hide in the bathroom to text Leo and Tinsley again. Neither have responded yet, but I feel like I should tell them what I'm about to do.

Me: *The police want me to tell them where the Sanderses are.*

I wait for a moment, and then the little reply bubble pops up.

Tinsley: *Do you know where they are?*

Me: *No, but I could tell them where we last saw them.*

Tinsley: *You mean lead them to the castle?*

Me: *Yes*

Tinsley: *Which means other people are going to end up knowing where it is. Before AJ can do anything?*

Leo: *You have to do it, Lin.*

Me: *Are you sure?*

Leo: *Yeah. You know how I feel about them, but they don't know what they're doing, and as we found out, that could be disastrous.*

Me: *Okay. You're right. Thanks, guys. I'll keep you posted.*

I shove my phone in my pocket and go outside to the picnic table where the adults are all waiting. I sit down and fold my hands on the table. "What do you want to know?"

They ask me a couple of questions about why the Sanderses followed us, which I explain was their own doing. "Aaron and Michael were bullying Leo and tried to go after him, like they have been doing for weeks, and the dogs knocked Aaron down. We never touched any of them."

Mr. Sanders looks only slightly uncomfortable at the mention of his kids going after Leo.

"So where did you last see them after that?"

I take a deep breath. "At the Castle in the Clouds."

The police look at me for a minute like they might think I'm joking. One of their faces squints like he's suppressing a laugh. Mr. Sanders's face lights up.

"I'm serious," I say. "It's actually up there. It's really hard to find, but we found it and so did your boys, Mr. Sanders, although my trail markers helped them until they stupidly removed half of them. Sorry, no offence, but it was a really bad decision. We were all there together like you said, but they followed us on their own."

"Then how'd you all get separated?" one officer asks.

I take a breath. "We knew we couldn't defend ourselves against them. They're too strong, and we were tired of being pushed around. So I made up a plan that we'd all race home and the winner got to claim the castle. They ran, but we stayed back."

The adults all look at one another and at me. No one seems all that surprised or angry. Not even Mr. Sanders. One of the officers nods. "You think you're strong enough to go up there again today?" he asks me.

My mom puts her hand on mine. "I don't know, Officer. I realize the gravity of the situation, but—"

"We'd go most of the way on ATVs," he says. "The rangers can take us up the service road. She won't have to walk all that much. We just need to know the last point of contact."

My parents still don't look convinced, but I know they have nothing else to go by to find those boys. I will at least recognize the surroundings, maybe even find a couple of scraps of red fabric. And no matter how horrible they are, they should get to come home.

"I can do it," I say. "I can at least show you how far up the mountain they went."

"Then we'll all go," my mom says. I look at her, surprised. "You wanted an adventure together, right?" she asks, sort of laughing. "I don't know what you were thinking, but you can at least show me what was worth the hike."

"I'd like that," I say. I'm pretty sure AJ wouldn't mind my parents seeing it. She seemed to think my mom sounded pretty cool, so maybe we'd even run into her. "You too, Dad?"

"Absolutely."

Within an hour, after we eat breakfast, I'm strapping on a helmet and getting on the back of a ranger's four-wheeler near the trailhead. Mom, Dad, and Mr. Sanders are on other vehicles, and the police and rangers take us about halfway up the mountain—as far as the service road goes, which is even closer to where I remember the sheer rock wall being. It's wild to think we could have walked this road for a much quicker ascent if we'd only known. But then we would have lost so much of the journey that was truly fun. I'm not sure I'd want to trade that part.

From there, we have to go on foot. But it's nowhere near as difficult as the first time up, when we were searching for landmarks and running from the Sanderses and hiding in the rain. It only takes me a short time to find one strip of red fabric tied to a branch.

"From here we have to go straight up and around this narrow ridge," I say, and our group heads in that direction.

"I'm proud of you," Dad says. "Red trail markers. Smart."

"I thought so too, until Aaron and Michael removed at least the first half of them."

My mom shakes her head. I can tell she has some choice words for the Sanders brothers, but she keeps her mouth shut. It only takes a little while to find our way back to the narrow path that heads up the steep side of the ridge to where the rock face and tunnel entrance are. I have a slight feeling of dread as we approach, like the magic of our discovery is all gone now. The castle will quickly become an often-visited site for sure, something people will paint their names on, leaving behind their campfires and trash just like at the ruins. Or like the Sanderses said, turned into a vacation spot. Either way, it's the end of a legend. A legend I thought I wanted to solve for myself, but instead I got to meet AJ, hear her story, and in a way I feel like I became part of it. I'm just afraid AJ won't be able to compete with the Sanders household if Mr. Sanders really intends to somehow buy it and turn it into a resort.

"This is a dead end," one of the police says, staring up at the giant rock face. "Are you sure we went the right way?"

The rock door is closed, and I know we didn't close it when we left. AJ's work, I'm sure. "Yes," I say, and walk over to where we uncovered the lever and gears to open the door. But the lever will not budge. "This weird contraption opens a door . . ." I press down on it as hard as I can but nothing happens. My dad tries to help, and still nothing.

"It must be jammed," I say. "But I swear the castle is right on the other side of this wall."

Mr. Sanders presses his hand on the rock and seems distracted.

"Huh," one of the rangers says. "Pretty sure that's an old lock system for a canal."

"What do you mean?" I ask.

"Down by the river, on the canal side, you see these a lot—gears and levers and such. They open locks—doors—to let water through." He examines the system. "Seems someone dragged one up here, or rebuilt it, maybe. It's definitely not working, though."

"But it *was* working," I say. "I swear it." I look at my parents. Dad shrugs. Mom puts a hand on my shoulder. I think they still believe me, and I can tell Mr. Sanders is interested, but the police officers definitely do not seem convinced.

"Either way, it doesn't really matter," I say. "This was the last place the boys would have been. They ran out from this tunnel, and then I don't know what direction they went."

One of the police radios to someone off the mountain. "We're at what we think is the last known sighting. Nope, no castle." Then he looks at us and says, "Okay, one of us is going to drive you back down and we will take it from here. Thank you for your help, miss."

"That's it?" I ask.

"That's enough," he says. "Now we can plan a much more thorough search, fanning out back down the mountain. The group on the ground will make their way to us, and hopefully along the way we will run into the boys. You've narrowed down our search area, and it's been much more help than you realize."

He motions for us to head back down, and so we do, one by one, back off the narrow ledge that leads to the rock face. Down the hill toward the service road where rangers are waiting to take us home. I was happy to help, maybe if nothing else just so I could go back up there and prove it's real to everyone. Now it feels like I'm officially leaving it all behind, unable to show my parents, or maybe anyone ever. And I have no idea where things stand with Leo and Tinsley and if we'll be able to hang out at all ever again.

It makes it all seem like a sad, fading dream.

Back at the bus, everything that was bubbling up bursts. Much louder than I intend, I shout, “I swear to you it’s there. You believe me, right?”

“Yes, of course we do,” Mom says, holding a hand up so I don’t get louder. “We can try again sometime.”

“I was just so excited for you to see it. So you’d know what we found.” Then I think, if Michael hadn’t stolen my camera, she could still see it, and it causes an instant ache in my gut. I have to fess up to that too. “Mom, there’s something I didn’t tell you.” But before I can there’s a loud knock on the door.

Dad says as he gets up to see who it is, “Now, who is this?”

I go over and peek. It’s AJ, wearing her signature cargo pants and hiking boots, and carrying a duffle bag and a giant brown box in her arms. “Oh my gosh! That’s AJ. That’s Anna Pace! Invite her in, Dad, she’s cool.”

Dad opens the door.

“Hi!” She sounds breathless. “I’m AJ.”

“So we’ve heard,” he says. “Come on—”

She comes in before he can finish and drops the duffle bag on the floor and the big box on the table, making quite a loud entrance.

"—in," Dad finishes.

AJ looks around the bus. "Wow. You'd never guess from the outside how cool this thing is."

"How did you know where to find me?" I ask.

"I'm a good tracker," she says, smirking. "And Jeffery Holiday and I go way back. Hope it's okay I stopped by?"

"Of course," Mom says. "We've only heard a little bit about you, but it's nice to meet you. Come sit and let me make you some coffee? Tea?"

"You don't have to go to no trouble," AJ says.

"For the woman who kept my baby safe, I'd brew way more than tea." Mom goes to the cabinet and starts pulling out all kinds of snacks. "Thank you for getting the kids home."

"Oh, that wasn't me," AJ says.

"No?" Dad asks. "Some other woman who lives in a castle?" he jokes.

"No, I mean, yes, I took them in for a night. But your daughter here got us home. She figured out a quicker route than I knew." She raises her hands. "I know, I was shocked too!"

Mom looks at me adoringly. "Is it true, Lin? You didn't mention that."

I just smile, and AJ says, "From what I hear, the apple doesn't fall too far from the tree."

We all sit down at the table, and AJ tells them everything

about her family, the sword, and the Freemasons. "Those Freemasons have held the clues to the real secret all along," she says. "And I couldn't figure it out until you three came in and destroyed my fireplace."

"Lin," Dad says. "You said you left everything untouched."

"Oh, it wasn't on purpose, right, Lin?" AJ winks at me.

"No! Not at all," I insist. "We were trying to figure out how to get AJ's attention," I explain to my parents. "And Leo accidently broke off a stone, and that led to another and another . . . and, well, we saw what we saw."

AJ opens the box on the table and shows the sword to my parents. It's even prettier that I remembered. It has runes and other inscriptions on the blade and hilt, and the initials *AP* really stand out now. "Tell me the truth. Is this Excalibur?" I whisper. "King Arthur's sword?"

My parents give me an odd look, but AJ smiles and says, "When I was growing up, my mom once told me we survive because of stories. She said some are true, some are myth, and some are legend."

Mom and Dad both sit back a little bit and listen. "What's the difference?" I ask.

"Truth is proven; myth is also proven, but to be false. And only legend can live forever."

"Why?"

"Because it's the truth that cannot be proven." AJ taps on the box. "People will always keep looking for answers, even just answers about their own personal truth. It's what keeps us going."

I think I understand mostly what she means, but maybe not totally. I nod, though, so she thinks I'm up to speed.

"We are seekers, by nature," Mom says, nodding for real. "Each one of us in our own little or big way."

"So, does that mean yes? You think this sword is part of the legend or no?" I ask.

AJ sips her tea and takes her time, which kills me. Finally she says, "I think legends start with truth. And I think my aunt had no idea how big of a story she was getting herself into when she stole this. But I don't know if we'll ever know who the original owner was. Just like we may never know who was buried with it."

I shudder at the memory. But I am now convinced this is King Arthur's sword. There are too many clues that lead in that direction to think otherwise, and I think AJ is just playing it safe until it's back in better protection. There'd be no other reason for such secrecy and cover-up. The erased articles, all the symbols, and the lengths people have gone to keep it hidden all point toward the real Excalibur and the legend of King Arthur. And it was in safe hands for centuries thanks to the Freemasons. Until however-many-greats Aunt Anna Pace inserted herself in the story.

And like all good legends, it continues to pick up characters along the way.

I start to tap my feet under the table. Mom puts a hand on my knee to try to settle me.

"Don't worry, I already reported that little skeletal surprise," AJ says, covering the sword back up. "And I'll be bringing this to the Freemasons, and hopefully persuading them to cough up my aunt's documents. Then we can decide together what to do with this beast."

"Will you promise to stay in touch and let us know what comes of all this?" my dad asks.

"Of course," AJ says, and writes down a post office box address for herself—all she has currently—and my parents give her our contact information. Meanwhile I can hardly sit still, and I hate to be rude, but I have to go talk to Leo and Tinsley.

"I have a huge favor to ask, and I know I've done a lot of things to make everyone mad, but can I please go check on my friends really quick? I'll come right home, I promise."

Mom looks a little perturbed at my request and says, "Honey, you have a guest right now."

But AJ waves her hand and starts gathering her things. "Heck no, I gotta run. But it's been great! I promise to be in touch. I might be in the market for one of these buses. This is a rad deal!" We all say goodbye, and AJ is gone as quickly as she arrived.

"Please?" I clasp my hands together in a desperate beg. "Twenty minutes tops."

Dad rubs his face and looks at Mom, who shakes her head and says sternly, "Twenty minutes." I kiss her on the cheek and run to Tinsley's as fast as I can.

She comes right out. She's dressed in yellow shorts and a T-shirt with a giant SpongeBob on it. "What is it?" she asks as I give her a huge hug. She hugs me back. "Is everything okay?"

"Yes! You? Are you in big trouble?" I ask.

"I'm grounded from TV and my phone, which is why it took me a while to text you back. I had to sneak it. Not sure when I'll be seeing it again," she says, but she doesn't look mad at all. "Between you and me: worth it."

"What did your dad think?"

Tinsley puts her hands on her heart. "You should have seen his face, Lin. Mom was all lecturing about going off without telling anyone, and I could see him behind her, so much pride on his face despite agreeing with Mom. He wants to know all the details now."

"Well, I have more for you. Are they mad at me?" I ask, terrified I might have ruined our friendship before it even had much of a chance to take flight. "Would they let you go with me to Leo's real quick?"

Her eyebrows knit together, but she looks intrigued. "Let me ask." And she dips in the door for a couple of minutes. I scuff my sneakers on the sidewalk, kicking gravel while I wait. Finally she comes back, and her mom is right behind her.

"Oh, hi, Mrs. Cooper. It's nice to meet you." I wrap my hands behind my back. Tinsley looks like a mini version of her mother, minus the pink hair.

"Lin?" Mrs. Cooper folds her arms in front of her. "It would have been nice to meet under other circumstances."

"I know, and I'm very, very sorry for that."

"Tinsley says now you want to steal her away again," she asks a little sternly, but she's also playful about it. I can tell I haven't ruined anything.

"Just real quick, ma'am," I say. "I want to tell her and Leo something, together. She'll be right back home. It'll only take a minute."

She looks at Tinsley, who gives her a huge, pleading grin, and says, "You have ten."

"Perfect." I take Tinsley's hand, thanking her mom as I run us both toward Leo's.

"What is going on?"

"We have to get Leo first."

At Leo's, I bang on the door until his mother answers. She has an actual stern look on her face and only holds the door half-open, like she's afraid I'm going to burst through it and kidnap her son. "I'm sorry, but he's resting," she says even though I can see him peeking out his bedroom window upstairs. "And I don't think you're the best influence for him right now."

"Please, Ms. Martin. I just have something really important to tell him. It will be very quick."

She shakes her head. "Go home." And slams the door.

I step back from the front porch. I guess I deserve this. But I'm not leaving without him at least knowing that he's now part of the legend he loves so much. I cup my hands over my mouth and scream as loud as I can.

"Leo Martin! You found the real Sword in the Stone!"

Every good adventure ends so a new adventure can start; maybe you'll find a mystery in your very own backyard, an adventure awaiting just outside your door.

Leo's mom eventually lets him hang out with us again. It takes a few days for her to soften, but really, it's a phone call from my dad that finally convinces her. He puts me on, and I apologize to her for coming up with the whole plan that put Leo in danger. At first she sounds really mad, but by the end of the conversation she says, "Well, I know that your friendship is really important to Leo. I've never seen him so happy. Just promise me you won't do something like this again?"

I promise her. I have no intentions of any more expeditions like this one, and if I'm even allowed to do more exploring this summer, I promise her that we will tell all the parents where we're going. And I mean it. Adventures don't have to be secret to be fun.

Aaron, Michael, and Seth are found later the same day the police had me help them. They're pretty beaten up from mosquitoes, scratches, and falls, and were extremely dehydrated and hungry. They all spend a night in the hospital but end up okay. We all feel much better when we know they are home safe. No one deserves to be lost or in danger. Maybe they've also learned a thing or two, like when a path is already marked for you, enjoy it, don't destroy it.

A few more days go by, and my mom begins talking about returning to the turtles. It brings that sinking feeling back in my stomach, but this time I'm okay with saying goodbye. I'm even okay with missing her because I know she's not leaving because she doesn't want to be with me. It won't be permanent, and now I have Leo and Tinsley. "Friends can become family too, Lin, if you open your heart up," she says. "Someday you'll probably realize that friends can even become home."

I like that idea. I always thought my family was only made up of our trio, the Three Musketeers forever. But there's no reason it can't be even bigger.

Newbridge has a giant Fourth of July festival every year, and this year they've invited AJ to speak about the castle and her family's longtime connection to town. While Newbridge can't grant ownership to her or anyone for the castle because it's technically now on state parkland, they are very happy they can officially update the town welcome sign to GATEWAY TO THE CASTLE IN THE CLOUDS. I know a lot of people are going to love hiking up there to see it, and hopefully take care of it—a little piece of history that Newbridge can finally claim to be part of.

Mr. Sanders never did or said anything about the castle as far as I know. Sometimes I wonder if he has some kind of plan up his sleeve, but Dad says the castle is protected by the state park status. Even Mr. Sanders can't buy the state of New Jersey.

One afternoon, about a week after our adventure, while Leo, Tinsley, and I are sitting at the picnic table and discussing the fate of both the castle and the sword, Seth shows up.

Leo immediately stands up. "What do you want?" Merlin and Little John jump up too. But they wag their tails. They're just happy to see people. Anytime, all the time.

Seth holds up a hand. "I only want to apologize. And return this." He hands me my mom's video camera. "It should be fine."

"Wow. Thank you." I take the camera. The battery is dead, but hopefully he's right.

He shoves his hands in his pockets. "Sorry. I would have returned it earlier, but it took a while to get it back from Michael."

"No, that's fine. I'm just really happy to have it," I say.

"It was really cool of you to help that day," he says to me. "We owe you our lives."

"Anyone would have done it," I say.

"Maybe." Seth shrugs. "Look, you guys should know that Sanders sent us up there after you."

"You mean *Mr.* Sanders?" I ask.

Seth nods. "Aaron and Michael showed him the map they took from you that day, and he told them to track you. Stupidly, I went along with it."

"What did he think would happen?" I ask.

"I honestly don't know. Between us, he's a control freak and orders them around like soldiers. He was probably just being nosy as usual, and he really did have all these wild ideas about buying the castle and getting rich off turning it into a hotel. But obviously that didn't work out. And this whole thing has changed Aaron and Michael."

It seems like Seth is telling the truth, but that's quite an order to give your kids—to head off into the woods alone. Although I'm sure Mr. Sanders had no idea they'd be gone that long. And I guess time will tell just how changed the brothers are.

"Anyway. Hope that thing still works for you."

He starts to go, and Leo calls out, "Hey, maybe we'll see you at school?"

Seth smiles. "Yeah. See you there." He waves and jogs away.

All three of us look at one another, stunned. "Wow," I say. "I wasn't expecting that."

"It was super nice, at least," Tinsley says. "Let's go see if it works! I want to see what you recorded!"

We run into the bus, plug in the camera, and hook it up to

my laptop. It pops right on. Everything is saved. I'm so happy I cover my face with my hands. "Come on, Lin," Leo says, "we want to see!" So I scroll through still photos and a few of the short videos of our adventure, each of us pointing out funny moments and laughing at how filthy we were. "Tinsley, your hair, though," I say. "Nothing beats it!"

"Pinkie always reigns," she says, claiming AJ's nickname for herself.

"These are great," I say. "I'm so glad it was saved so I'll always have this to look back on when I leave—" I stop myself. The words flew out of my mouth before I even thought about it, and I'm not even sure how I feel about leaving or staying anymore. So much has changed in just a few weeks. I kind of want both. But I know I can't, at least not right now. I just have to wait and see what's up the road.

Leo and Tinsley look at me. "What?" I ask.

"You look like something's wrong," Tinsley says.

"It's just—you know we don't stay in one place very long," I say. "I mean, I think I'll get to finish seventh grade here, but by then my mom will be back for good. And they will probably finish up the house, and after that . . . wherever we go next is up to them."

"You'll be happy to be back on the road," Leo says, looking at the table. "Back to a more exciting life."

"Yeah. Mostly, I guess." I have been imagining what it would be like to stay, though. To go through the rest of middle school and high school with Leo and Tinsley. To go to dances and football games and parties together. Graduate together. All that seems really far away, and I've never really thought about it before. I never thought it was something I wanted. But sitting here with them makes me miss it even though it hasn't happened yet. "So far this is a pretty exciting life too," I say.

I play a video I took from one of the windows overlooking the castle's courtyard. So many people will be posting videos like this soon. But I have the original. And even though AJ was there first, way before us, I still feel like we made a major discovery, and a journey I could never have done without Leo and Tinsley. Which makes me realize exactly what my movie will be about.

We're quiet as I skip through the remainder of the photos. I'm already forming a plan in my head about how I will edit the videos together, with still shots thrown in. I'm going to need a little help from Mom, but I'll narrate over some of it, tell our story, and talk a little about the legend. It should all come together pretty easily, and Leo and Tinsley will be so surprised. Toward the end there's half a dozen photos of Aaron, Michael, and Seth, who clearly had fun with the camera after they stole it. They're actually pretty funny, posing in goofy positions, hanging from tree branches, even throwing leaves in the air like little kids.

"Are you going to delete those?" Leo asks.

"I don't know. I think I might be able to use them."

The last few photos we look at are the ones Michael took of us right before we were going to fight them.

"Oh. My . . . ," Tinsley says, covering her mouth to keep from cracking up.

Leo leans in for a closer look, and his eyes get wide. "Is *that* what I really looked like?"

"That's what we *all* really looked like," I say. The three of us look like we're ready for battle. Covered in dirt and leaves, even blood, our hair sticking up in all directions, and each of us holding weapons. It's the expressions on our faces that really stand out, though. It reminds me how desperate and afraid we were, and yet together we were unified and brave.

By the Fourth of July, Mom has left to finish out her turtle expedition, and it's just me and Dad again. I miss her already, but I've been busy editing not only a special movie about our quest, but a series of YouTube videos that I want to upload into my own channel about survival in the woods just for kids. I haven't had a lot of time to think too much about missing her. She helped me get going with the editing software, and I can't wait to show her how I finished it up. She won't be able to watch each episode as I load them, but she promised to catch up as soon as she could. It's funny how my plan was to send her a movie about how horrible my life was going without her, and instead I made a movie of how much fun I had. And how she was sort of with me the entire time anyway. It feels like I'm connected to her while still doing my own thing—and that's a brand-new, but really wonderful feeling. I'm still going to send it to her after I'm done. But first, I have a very special plan for it.

Yesterday I walked to town early, before Leo and Tinsley

were probably even out of bed. It was already very warm and humid, but I didn't mind. I reached the municipal building right as they were opening for the day and introduced myself to Mayor Pete, who agreed to my plan.

"You know, everyone is pretty amazed at how you kids found that castle," Mayor Pete said. "I mean, honestly, I've lived here my entire life and I've never gone looking. I don't know anyone who has. Most people didn't think it really existed."

"You can't find anything interesting if you don't go looking," I said.

He laughed. "Yes, I suppose you're right." He tucked the little travel drive I gave him into a big envelope. "I'll take good care of this."

Today is Newbridge's Fourth of July town-wide festival and fireworks display—something else I've never done. It goes for most of the day with live music, tons of food trucks, a parade, tents with arts and crafts, and all kinds of vendors selling everything from honey to jewelry. All over town, stores have tables of sale items out, business displays, and more. There's something new to look at in every direction.

"Where did all these people even come from?" I ask Leo and Tinsley as we walk around town. We already got ice cream from Dilly's, and now we're heading to the park. But it's crowded on the sidewalks, and we have to squeeze our way through everyone to get anywhere.

"Everyone comes out for these things," Tinsley says.

"I like it," I say.

We spend the entire day at the park lying on a blanket and listening to the music. Leo brought a Frisbee, so we toss that back and forth too, and play with the dogs. Dad comes by with some lunch, but then he sits with Leo's mom and Mr. Holiday and a few other people he's befriended for the main ceremony.

"My mom said she might try to get my dad out today. Someone donated a new wheelchair for him," Tinsley says as she looks around the crowd.

"Oh, that's awesome," I say. "Is he feeling better?"

"He's getting there," she says. "Mom says one day at a time. He's been in a way better mood since hearing about the castle and knowing it's protected by the state. I thought he'd be upset that AJ was years ahead of all of us, but he wasn't at all. He seemed relieved and asked me to describe it twice. He still won't tell me anything about the Freemasons, though."

"A loyal member," I say. "It's kind of cool, actually."

Mayor Pete gets up on the bandstand stage and welcomes everyone to the event. "First on the agenda this evening is a special presentation by Miss Anna Pace," he says, and then motions for AJ to come up on the stage. We haven't seen her since the day she stopped by with the sword. She carries a wooden box with her, and I notice she's wearing a pin that has the same symbol as the Freemason lodge. I point it out to Tinsley. "Do you think they inducted her in as a member? The first woman Freemason?"

Tinsley's eyes light up. "Maybe! I think you might be right!"

Everyone claps, and when they are quiet, she says, "Thank you, truly. But I want to thank you, Newbridge, in advance, as you are now the gateway to and keeper of the castle that has been in my family for generations. As some of you know, I'd been poking around town for years."

There's some light laughter in the crowd, and she continues. "I always wanted my great-aunt's legacy to be known, but there were some who, unbeknownst to me at the time, wanted the castle's location protected until we knew for sure whether or not this was still in it." She opens the wooden box and shows the sword. A wave of "ohhhh" ripples over the crowd. "Well, they were right. It was."

More laughter. I know the "they" she's talking about is the Freemasons, but I wonder why she doesn't mention them by name. She *must* be one of them now, and that's why she's wearing that pin and has sort of spun her story about who was protecting what. I suppose working with the secret keepers is better than working against them. As long as the secrets are good. And these seem to be good.

"I'm going to be returning this greatsword to the Lodge of King Arthur in Scotland, where my aunt stole it from, and they will likely be donating it to a local museum. It's from the thirteenth century, and I imagine she brought it here hoping it would end up providing for her needs as she started out in a new country. How it ended up in her glorious castle's fireplace, we may never know. I plan to right that wrong, but I think it's important to remember that even though she may not have had all the best intentions, or make the best decisions, she still made a great achievement."

The audience gives her a loud round of applause. Leo, Tinsley, and I all grin from ear to ear, and my hands hurt from clapping so hard.

"One last thing, before I run off this godforsaken stage, is that I want to thank the people who actually made this possible. Melinda Moser, Tinsley Cooper, and Leo Martin, will you please come up here?"

All three of us look at one another. None of us were expecting this. Not that there's an actual Freemason lodge named for King Arthur, or that AJ would honor us! All eyes are on us as we stand and make our way up to the stage. AJ positions us in a line facing the crowd. "I present to you the explorers who actually found the sword. All your names will be part of the display."

The crowd claps and whistles, and I look at AJ. She nods and smiles at me. I can't believe it's true. My name on a real discovery. I look out at the crowd and see my dad standing and trying to clap his heart out, while also trying to hold his phone to video us, which is why he's not the photographer in the family. Leo's mom and even Tinsley's parents in the back are all clapping for us. My dad has a proud grin on his face that tells me he knew all about this. They must have all known.

When everyone settles, AJ lets each of us hold the sword for photos. People take a ton of them, and I feel like a superstar. I notice, in the way back of the crowd, even the Sanders brothers are standing and clapping too.

After the photos, AJ carefully wraps the sword and places it back in the wooden box. I want to ask her if she's in with the Freemasons now because I don't know if I'll see her again, but I can't follow her right now, because it's time for my part of the presentation. Leo and Tinsley start to leave the stage, but when I don't follow, they stop. "Are you coming?" Leo asks.

"In a second," I say. "You go ahead."

They're confused, but then Mayor Pete takes the microphone back and says, "And now we have a special presentation from one of our young explorers herself, Miss Lin Moser." He hands me the microphone, and the crowd claps again.

"Thank you, everyone," I say. "I, uh—as a lot of you know, my family travels all over the country."

"We love your show!" someone shouts from the crowd.

"Oh! Thank you," I say, grinning. "Well, I've learned a lot about making videos and movies from my parents, and I decided when we moved here, I was going to make my own. Originally, I wasn't happy about being here. But there are two people who made what I thought was going to be the worst summer into the very best summer anyone could have, and we're just getting started. So, this film is dedicated to Leo and Tinsley."

Leo and Tinsley are still standing on the side of the stage, so shocked they don't move. Leo's face is quickly turning pink, and Tinsley clasps her hands together and puts them under her chin. Surprised, but smiling.

I nod to the guy who's going to run the projector, and he flips it on. I sit down on the edge of the stage while the film plays. The title pops on first, and adventurous soundtrack music plays in the background. I can't help but watch Leo's and Tinsley's faces to see their reactions.

One Terrible Summer

BY LIN MOSER

Leo and Tinsley look at me, surprised and confused about my title choice, but then the movie plays and their attention goes back to the screen. It's only ten minutes long, but took me a lot of hours to put together, and although I was happy with it, I felt like I could have tweaked it forever.

It starts with the camera on the scribbled bathroom door:

LOVE YOURSELF, YOU'RE STUCK WITH HER TILL THE END

And my voice-over of how I was feeling about moving to Newbridge and missing out on my mom's trip, being left behind because I wasn't adventurous enough for her anymore. Definitely not loving myself or my situation so much. Then it goes to us before we really knew much about one another, my interviews and attempted interviews with Leo where he looks like a deer in the headlights, and then little clips of our entire hiking expedition—the montage I had planned from the beginning. There's Merlin and Little John, the Sanderses and Seth, the majestic buck in the woods, and of course a lot of incredible mountain and castle footage, which is the crowd's favorite part. They gasp and ooh and aah at every scene.

The best part, though, in my opinion, is as the movie plays, you can see all our faces change from awkward and a little sad at first, to relaxed and laughing even during the scary times in the woods. In the beginning we keep a safe distance, and by the end we lean into one another, laughing and comfortable. It's the story of a friendship, more than the story of a castle. The story of how home is people, not a place. My mom taught me that.

At the very end, I made a short animation that shows the title with the word *terrible* being erased, and *outstanding* written in with a Sharpie.

When it's over, every single person in the park stands up. Screams and applause and more whistling nearly deafens me. I'm pretty sure there are tears in my dad's eyes.

Tinsley runs up onstage and hugs me tight. "That was amazing!"

Leo looks a little shy about the whole thing, but he comes back with her. At first I think he's going to shake my hand or something, but then he hugs me too and the crowd really goes wild. "I'm going to get you for this," he teases.

"Did you like it?" I ask.

"I loved it."

After everyone calms down and the mayor thanks me again, we jump off the stage and make our way back to our blanket. Dad gives me a big hug and says how impressed he is. "Your mom told me the two of you were working on this together before she left, but I had no idea how involved it was. We're putting that up on the channel, don't you think? Talk about content!"

"Yes, that would be so cool, Dad!" I truly love this idea. Now instead of tagging along, I'll actually get to take an active part. My own part.

"Okay, done! Now you have some more fans to attend to," he says as he backs away.

Then a bunch of people I don't know congratulate me—all three of us—for what we did.

A lady introduces herself as one of the teachers at the high school. "I know you have a couple years yet, but we have a film club at the high school that you would be a perfect fit for!"

"Oh," I say, a little unsure how to respond. "Thank you? That's . . . great." I glance over at Dad, who seems to say "sorry." I'm not sure if I was hoping for him to say, "We'll stay forever!" or not. I don't tell the teacher that I might not be here for high school. My life is unpredictable. But it's mine, and I love it.

"You never know what might happen," Leo says quietly as we sit down, his shoulder against mine, Tinsley on my other side. I didn't realize he noticed the conversation with the teacher, but he smiles. "Maybe your parents will find another house here to work on and you can stay."

"Maybe they can do the castle!" Tinsley says. "That would take a decade at least. Could you imagine if that happened and you got to live there?"

"We never live in the houses they flip," I say. "And you already know it belongs to the state."

"Just *pretend* for five minutes," Tinsley says. "You can do that, right? You can pretend? Close your eyes."

"Tinsley."

"Just do it!"

I close my eyes. She says, "Imagine sleepovers in that giant ballroom, you know, after they fix the floor you fell through and the fireplace Leo destroyed, and your sweet sixteen party. Long tables with colorful fabrics of silk and lace, and silver platters of fruit and chocolate. Candles of all heights down the center, a roaring fire, garlands of roses and herbs—"

"I have to admit, this does sound amazing."

"And maybe someday, you'd even get married there."

I open my eyes. "That's funny. But none of this is happening anyway. Fortunately my dad is not selling the house early to Mr. Sanders, so I have one guaranteed year. We get one year. And after that we don't know."

That quiets all three of us.

Leo picks at a fuzz on the blanket. "You know, a year is a

long time. Especially in dog years." Which makes me laugh since it's the same thing I said to my mom.

But he's right—we have plenty of time, and since I wasn't grounded for life and just have to tell my dad whenever I want to go anywhere, who's to say there isn't a little adventure we could go on?

Leo continues, "And we still have *all* summer break left. We should make the most of it before school starts."

"What do you have in mind?" Tinsley asks. "Rereading *The Sword in the Stone* for the ten thousandth time?"

Leo throws the fuzz at Tinsley. "No. I was thinking about that rumor about the old quarry."

Tinsley tries to cover my ears. "Don't even get her started!"

I dodge her. "What are you talking about?"

"Apparently it used to be a gemstone mine."

I suddenly remember the book in the library: *The Legend of the Quarry*. There were a few interesting books in there, come to think of it. "Gems in New Jersey?"

"Yep. Opals and rubies even."

Tinsley gives Leo a playful shove. "How do you know this?"

"Because unlike some of us, I listen in class instead of plugging music in my ears," he says, and shoves her back.

I put a hand on both of them. "Okay, enough. So, you're telling me there's an old quarry that may or may not have opals and rubies in it? Here? In Newbridge?"

Leo nods and grins. Tinsley throws herself back on the

blanket, puts her arms over her face, and groans. "Lin, you've created a monster!"

I mean, we do have eight weeks left of summer.

Might as well go find some adventure.

After dark, the fireworks display begins. The three of us lie on our backs on the blanket. I'm in the middle, and I hold both Tinsley's and Leo's hands. In the dark, no one seems to be bothered by it. The colorful explosions overhead distract me for a little bit, taking my mind off the fact that in less than a year I will have to say goodbye to the two best friends I could have ever hoped to have. It's weird to think that only a few months before this night, I was missing the life I had on the road and now I'm already missing this new life being settled in Newbridge and I haven't even left it yet.

It makes me wonder how my parents have done this for so long. How AJ does it. Or how Annie Smith Peck did it way back then. How did she travel the world, especially in her time before the internet and cell phones made it easy to stay in touch with friends and family? How could she leave people behind every time to chase after a new mountain?

Was the climb really worth it?

I look at Leo and Tinsley and think, if she ever made friends as good as these two, then yes, the climb was worth it. Because friends like this last a lifetime, no matter where you make your home.

ACKNOWLEDGMENTS

To my incredibly talented and tenacious agent of six years(!), Linda Epstein: I cannot express enough how much your encouragement, suggestions, and professional prowess have meant to me.

And my editor, Melissa Warten: Thank you for believing in me and this story, and making me dig so much deeper than I originally thought it was meant to go. I love what we created together. And thank you to everyone on the FSG team. I'm proud to be part of such a great imprint full of hardworking, dedicated, and timely people.

To Ricardo Bessa: When they told me who was designing this cover, I of course scrambled to Instagram to see whose hands my "baby" would be in, and I was SO excited when I saw your work. The D&D piece, in particular, confirmed you were the absolute perfect artist for this project. This is my sixth book and when I saw the final art, it was the first time I actually cried over a cover! Thank you for capturing my "kids" so well.

A special thank-you for input from friends Melissa Bigelli and Kerri Tollinger for help with names for the famous YouTube parents, and Freemason "secrets," respectively.

People ask authors all the time where they get their inspiration from, or if characters are based on real people, and this is the first story I've written where I pulled from a much more personal place to do exactly that. I intentionally infused some of the best characteristics from my own life and my most favorite people and it was SO MUCH FUN. Tinsley is lightly based on my daughter, Ainsley, who, from a very young age and into adulthood, has loved dressing as characters. When she was young she'd go to school in costumes, wigs, makeup, the works! And I never wanted to squelch that creativity, but I did have to draw the line at red pleather stilettos in fifth grade. Sorry, kiddo. But you can wear them now if you want! Thank you for letting me use your creative spirit and loyal friendship for this story. To my boys . . . more stories are coming, so don't think you're safe. To all three of you: Thank you for loving me as your mom, and understanding me as best you could, even when I wasn't always there.

My parents gave me two incredible gifts: books and nature. When I was in my twenties and struggling with trying to figure out who I was and what to be when I grew up, my grandfather said, "Think about what you loved as a child." Here I am, two decades later, and *The Hike to Home* is just one expression of that genius advice, but certainly encompasses so many of my loves. Thank you, family, for allowing me the